La Esmeralda Del Tiempo

A Novel
Copyright, 2025, All Rights Reserved
By Jeffrey Estrella
AI assisted with the novel

Part 1: The Unseen Struggle

Chapter 1: Shadows in Chronix Bay

- Introduce Isabella Monteverdi: undocumented, cautious, working under the table in a laundromat.
- Establish Chronic Bay as a gritty NYC suburb with an oppressive atmosphere.
- She avoids ICE raids, deals with a landlord's threats, and clings to her dream of studying history.

"Immigration is not just a link between worlds, it's a bridge to a better future." Anonymous

Chapter 1: Shadows in Chronic Bay

The laundromat buzzed with a tired hum—the kind that settled in the bones after too many years of silence. Isabella Monteverdi moved between machines like a ghost, her faded jeans dusted with lint and her black hoodie pulled tight over her head. Outside, Chronic Bay simmered in the late September heat, the smell of salt and exhaust clinging to the air like regret.

It was almost 11 p.m., and she was still on her feet. The boss had asked her to cover the late shift again. No papers, no union, no protections—just a nod and a whispered "sí, señor" so she could keep the job another week. He didn't know her name. He called her "Chica."

She pushed a heavy cart filled with damp clothes, her hands raw and chapped from detergent and bleach. Every so often, she'd glance up at the security camera near the entrance. It wasn't working—it hadn't for months—but habits like checking didn't die easy.

A mother with a crying toddler shuffled out, leaving the place nearly empty. Good. Fewer eyes meant fewer questions.

Isabella stepped outside, letting the door shut behind her with a thud. She lit a cigarette, holding it between fingers that trembled just slightly. Down the block, red and blue lights danced silently through the mist. ICE raids had been happening more often lately. She didn't know who they'd taken this time, but she'd heard the screaming three nights ago.

She inhaled. Held. Released.

This wasn't the life she'd imagined when she crossed the border six years ago. She had dreamed of libraries and coffee shops, of college lectures on ancient civilizations and notebooks filled with her own writing. She had been the top of her class back in Zacatecas—head always buried in books, dreaming about time and myth and the lost cities of the Maya.

Instead, she washed socks in Chronic Bay.

Still, there was something inside her that hadn't died yet. A flicker. A hope so stubborn it refused to drown, even under debt, fear, and fading dreams.

Her phone buzzed in her pocket. A message from Lucia, her friend from the shelter.
"Careful tonight. Rumors of ICE at the Roosevelt stop."
She typed back: **"I'm okay. Just finishing. Be safe."**

The wind picked up suddenly, swirling trash down the sidewalk. Isabella turned her face from it, but not before she noticed something strange in the alley across the street.

A figure.

Still. Watching.

She blinked. The figure was gone.

The wind died. The hum of the laundromat returned.

She crushed her cigarette beneath her boot and went back inside.

The laundromat's back room was small, lined with broken machines, old detergent boxes, and forgotten clothes. Isabella sat on an overturned bucket, opened her bag, and pulled out the small leather-bound book she carried everywhere—a journal and a secret. Its cover was worn, corners curled, pages filled with half-translated glyphs, sketches, and questions.

She flipped to a page titled **"The Esmeralda de Tiempo."**

A myth. A story her abuela used to tell her on stormy nights, when candles flickered and wind rattled the shutters. The Esmeralda was said to be a stone of emerald, warm to the touch, carved with ancient symbols. A gift from the gods—or maybe a curse. It was said to twist time, to unravel fate, to open doors that should have stayed shut.

It was nonsense. But also... not.

In recent weeks, Isabella had begun finding symbols around Chronic Bay—etched into subway tunnels, tagged on alley walls, scratched onto streetlamps. The same ones from the codex. They matched the glyphs in her book. She didn't believe in coincidence anymore.

"Someone's trying to tell me something," she whispered.

Or maybe she was losing her mind.

She didn't have time to spiral. The front door jingled.

Isabella shoved the book into her bag and stood up, heart thudding.

A man had entered. He was tall, clean-cut, dressed in a navy suit. Not a customer. Not someone from the neighborhood. His shoes were too polished.

Isabella's instincts screamed: **run.**

Instead, she forced herself forward, putting on the fake smile she kept stored for moments like this.

"Lo siento, we're closing soon," she said, her voice tight.

The man didn't move. Didn't blink. "Isabella Monteverdi?"

She froze.

"I don't know who that is."

He smiled—but it didn't reach his eyes. "Wrong answer."

The man reached inside his coat.

Isabella didn't wait. She spun, grabbed her bag, and ran out the back door, feet slamming against concrete. The night exploded behind her—shouts, footsteps, the sound of something tearing through space.

She didn't look back. Not yet.

She just ran.

By the time she stopped, her lungs burned and her legs trembled. She crouched behind a rusted dumpster two blocks away, chest rising and falling like thunder.

What the hell was that?

She peeked around the corner. No one. Just the broken city, the flicker of broken lights, and the quiet rhythm of her heartbeat.

She pulled out the journal again.

And this time, she noticed something new.

A green glow, faint and pulsing, rising from the page—right where the glyph for "Time" had been inked.

The Esmeralda de Tiempo was real.

And someone else was looking for it.

Chapter 2: Invisible Wounds

- Flashback to her border crossing.

- Her trauma, resourcefulness, and isolation are revealed.

- She volunteers at a local church shelter—her only sanctuary.

Chapter 2: The Mark of the Stone

Isabella didn't sleep that night.

She made it back to her apartment just before sunrise, ducking through alleyways and slipping behind dumpsters. Her building—more of a crumbling box than a home—stood at the edge of Chronic

Bay's industrial district, where the air smelled like rust and the walls leaked when it rained. Rent was paid in cash and silence.

Inside, she bolted the locks, pulled down the blackout curtains, and peeled off her soaked hoodie. Her hands were still shaking.

She dropped her bag onto the warped kitchen counter and opened it, pulling out the leather-bound journal. The glow was gone.

But something else had changed.

On the inside of her left wrist, just above the snake tattoo she'd gotten at sixteen to feel brave, a new mark had appeared—faint, green, and glowing like fire under the skin. A symbol.

The same symbol from the journal.

Isabella's breath caught in her throat. She touched it with trembling fingers. It didn't hurt. It didn't feel like anything.

But it was there.

And it meant the story was real.

The Esmeralda de Tiempo.

She turned back to the journal and flipped through the pages again—looking for anything, any clue, any key. In the back, there was a passage her abuela had always whispered, but it had never made sense to her before.

"He who touches the Esmeralda touches the blood of gods. But beware: the stone does not belong to one person. It belongs to time. And time always demands balance."

Balance.

She had no idea what that meant, but it sounded like a warning. And judging by the man in the laundromat with the dead eyes and the weapon hidden in his coat, others were already searching.

And they were closer than she thought.

By mid-morning, Isabella was walking across the city with her hoodie pulled low and a burner phone clutched in her pocket. She needed help—but not just anyone. Not someone who'd call the police or ask for ID.

She needed Liberty.

She found the kid in an abandoned train yard behind an old electronics recycling plant. Liberty Wilson was hunched over the stripped shell of a subway car, typing furiously on a laptop balanced atop a crate, surrounded by hacked routers, tangled cords, and snack wrappers.

"You're two hours early," Liberty said without looking up. "And you look like someone tried to erase you with fire."

Isabella didn't smile. "Someone came for me last night. I think he knew my name."

Now Liberty looked up.

And then down.

"Is that glowing?"

Isabella pulled back the sleeve. The symbol shimmered faintly under the daylight.

Liberty whistled low. "Okay, so... we're officially in *weird* territory."

"You think?"

Liberty closed the laptop. "All right, spill it. Start from the beginning. No skips."

So she did. The laundromat. The glyphs. The strange man. The journal. The stone. The glow.

Liberty listened, fingers steepled beneath their chin, eyes calculating. Then they stood, turned, and pulled open a locked cabinet built into the train car's side.

From it, they retrieved a thin book wrapped in foil and twine—like something illegal and precious.

"I've seen that symbol," Liberty said. "Not just on your wrist. I found it inside an old quantum encryption script buried in the city's power grid. I thought it was just a signature."

Isabella blinked. "A what?"

"A signature. Like someone saying *I was here.* But I couldn't trace it. Every time I tried, the signal bent—like it moved. Through time."

Isabella stepped back. "That's not possible."

Liberty grinned. "Neither is glowing tattoos."

Touché.

They opened the book and flipped to a page lined with diagrams. "This is the one I traced. Same symbol. It showed up in five different places over the past hundred years—same shape, same placement, same decay pattern."

"Decay?"

"Energy signature. Like radiation, but weirder. Wilder. Almost... alive."

Isabella's head swam. "What does it mean?"

Liberty looked up. "It means you're not the first. And if that guy from last night really works for whoever's chasing this thing—"

"They already know I have it," Isabella finished.

Liberty nodded. "And that means we've got maybe twenty-four hours before someone tries again. Harder."

Back in the shadows of Chronic Bay, a man in a navy suit sat on the edge of a rooftop, fingers stained with old ink and blood. The briefcase beside him hummed with unnatural energy.

His eyes were cold.

His name was Malcolm Rutherford.

And the Time Stone's activation meant only one thing.

She had touched it.

And now, the clock had started.

Chapter 3: Whispers of the Past

•   Isabella finds an old codex hidden in a thrift store donation box.

•   The codex references the "Esmeralda de Tiempo," a legendary Mayan artifact said to defy time.

•   She begins researching.

Chapter 3: The Algorithm of Time

The train yard felt colder now.

Even in the glow of Liberty's hacked space heaters and flickering monitors, Isabella shivered. Maybe it was the adrenaline wearing off—or maybe it was the sense that something ancient had awakened and was watching.

Liberty paced back and forth, muttering to themselves as they scrolled through data streams on their laptop. The screen blinked with strings of green code, a digital heartbeat pulsing in time with Isabella's anxiety.

"You said the guy had silver eyes?" Liberty asked.

"Not silver—dead," Isabella corrected. "Like metal, but... wrong. Cold. Like they'd seen things no human should."

Liberty didn't respond. Instead, they clicked open a window and zoomed in on a blurred security still from the laundromat. It was grainy, but the figure was there—tall, expressionless, and cloaked in shadows.

No eyes visible. But the timestamp flickered.

11:11 p.m.
11:10 p.m.
11:09 p.m.
11:12 p.m.

It looped.

"What the hell?" Isabella leaned in. "It's reversing."

Liberty nodded grimly. "The feed's corrupted. That doesn't just happen. Someone—*something*—reached backward. Just a few seconds. Just enough to cover their tracks."

"Can people even do that?"

"No," Liberty said. "But *someone* with access to a Class 7 ChronoKey could."

Isabella blinked. "A what?"

"A device. Hypothetical. Black site tech. Stuff not even DARPA admits exists."

"How do you know all this?"

Liberty shrugged. "I have a hobby."

Across town, inside a glass tower built like a blade into the skyline, Judge Malcolm Rutherford stood in a courtroom empty of jurors and full of secrets.

The walls were soundproofed. The lights were custom-dimmed. The bailiff wasn't a bailiff—he was an armed operative from a task force known only to those who funded it.

On the judge's desk sat the briefcase.

Rutherford unlatched it slowly. The inside glowed faint green.

Not the Stone itself—he didn't have that. Not yet.

But a *fragment*. A splinter of what the Stone had been before it was broken and scattered across time.

It was enough.

He touched it, and time bent—just slightly, just enough to blur the air and make the clock on the wall twitch backward half a second.

He smiled.

"She's activated it," he said.

The man across from him, face hidden behind a scanner mask, nodded once. "We believe she made contact in Sector 7 of Chronic Bay."

"Does she know?"

"She suspects."

"Good," Rutherford said. "Let her. Fear is an excellent teacher."

The man hesitated. "Shall we extract her?"

Rutherford turned his cold gaze toward the skyline.

"No. We let her run. We let her *think* she has control. The Stone reacts to intent. If she tries to use it, even once, we'll trace it. When she opens the door, *we* will walk through it."

He closed the briefcase with a soft click.

"And then, time will belong to us."

Back at the train yard, Liberty was still piecing together data while Isabella sipped cold coffee and tried not to break down. Everything in her life had shifted in the span of a single night. Her reality was unraveling.

"I can't do this," she muttered.

Liberty looked up. "You already are."

"I'm just a waitress, Liberty. An undocumented waitress in a city that barely wants me alive. How the hell am I supposed to stop *that*?" She pointed to the looping security footage.

"You're not supposed to," Liberty said gently. "But you touched the Stone. That means it *chose* you. And maybe that means you're more than just a waitress."

Isabella didn't answer.

But somewhere deep inside, something stirred.

Resolve.

Not because she was ready. But because she didn't have the luxury of not being ready anymore.

"Okay," she said. "What's the next move?"

Liberty grinned. "We find the person who wrote this." They held up the journal. "There's a name scribbled in the margin—faded, but traceable. 'C. Z.'"

Isabella narrowed her eyes. "Camazotz?"

Liberty's grin faltered.

"You know that name?"

Isabella nodded slowly. "It's not a name. It's a god. An ancient Mayan god of death."

And just like that, the air shifted.

The Stone in her bag pulsed once—like a heartbeat.

Part 2: Discovery

Chapter 4: The Watcher in the Shadows

• She's followed. Camazotz appears, revealing himself as the guardian of the Esmeralda.

- He tests Isabella's moral compass before revealing more.

Chapter 4: The Keeper Beneath the City

The subway tunnels under Chronic Bay weren't listed on any public maps.

At least, not the ones Liberty showed Isabella.

"These were carved during the Great Expansion," Liberty explained, holding a tablet that flickered with blueprints. "Some were converted into smuggling routes, others abandoned after cave-ins. But here…" They tapped a point glowing red. "This section was sealed. Sealed and *scrubbed*—digitally erased."

"Why?"

"That's what we're going to find out."

They entered through an old metro access shaft behind the burned-out ruins of an old public library. Isabella ducked under fallen beams, stepping carefully across the cracked cement. Her bag was slung over her shoulder, the Time Stone tucked inside, pulsing faintly now—always faintly. Like it was aware.

Liberty dropped down into the tunnel first, flashlight clipped to their shoulder.

The air down there was thick with dust and something older— something almost alive.

"Remind me again what we're looking for?" Isabella asked.

"A man who shouldn't exist," Liberty replied. "According to the journal, 'C.Z.' is a guardian. A scribe. A witness to time."

"And you think he's down here?"

"I think if he's anywhere, it's somewhere people stopped looking a long time ago.

They walked for an hour.

The silence grew heavier the deeper they went. Graffiti gave way to ancient carvings—symbols like the one on Isabella's wrist etched into the walls. She ran her fingers across one.

It was warm.

Suddenly, the Stone flared inside her bag. A bright green flash, like a flare behind her eyes.

Isabella stumbled.

The walls around her rippled.

"Did you see that?" she gasped.

Liberty turned, wide-eyed. "Yeah."

The tunnel ahead was gone.

In its place was a door—massive, stone, and pulsing with emerald veins.

The Time Stone pulsed in response.

"Guess this is it," Liberty whispered.

Isabella stepped forward, lifted the Stone from her bag, and placed it into the carved socket in the door's center.

It clicked.

The door *breathed*.

Then it opened.

Inside was not a tunnel.

It was a temple.

Ancient stone pillars spiraled toward an impossible ceiling of stars, constellations neither of them recognized. The floor was lined with glowing glyphs that pulsed in rhythm with the Stone. At the far end of the chamber stood a figure—tall, robed, face hidden by a jaguar-shaped mask.

"Welcome," the figure said, voice like wind over bone. "Daughter of the Forgotten. Bearer of the Esmeralda."

Isabella's hand curled instinctively around the Stone.

"Who are you?"

The figure stepped forward. Removed the mask.

He looked human—but only just. His skin was deeply weathered, eyes ancient and knowing, hair tied in a long braid streaked with white and obsidian.

"I am called many things," he said. "But once, long ago, they called me Camazotz."

Isabella froze.

Liberty gasped.

"You're a god," Liberty whispered.

"A myth," Isabella said, her voice hoarse.

Camazotz nodded. "Both. Neither. I am a remnant. A guardian of balance. And you"—he looked at Isabella—"have disrupted it."

Isabella clenched her jaw. "I didn't ask for this."

"No one does," Camazotz said. "But now you carry the weight of time. And it is no longer still."

Camazotz led them deeper into the sanctuary, explaining what little he could—or what little he would.

The Time Stone, he said, was one of seven. The Esmeralda de Tiempo was not just a relic; it was a fulcrum. A hinge upon which countless futures turned.

"Others will come," he warned. "Some to take it. Some to end it. And one who seeks to become it."

"Judge Rutherford," Isabella muttered.

Camazotz's eyes narrowed. "That name should not be spoken in this place."

"He's hunting me."

"He's hunting *all* of us."

Liberty leaned in. "So what do we do?"

Camazotz reached into his robes and drew out a key—a simple piece of obsidian carved with glowing runes.

"You learn," he said, handing it to Isabella. "Before you can wield the Stone, you must understand what it *costs*."

"Cost?" Isabella echoed.

Camazotz's face darkened. "Time is not a gift. It is a *currency*. Every action you take echoes through centuries. Every step forward steals something from the past."

The sanctuary began to shake—just slightly.

Camazotz looked up, alarmed. "They've found us."

"Who?" Liberty asked.

Camazotz turned to Isabella. "The ones who serve Rutherford. The ones he's *rewritten*."

"What do we do?" Isabella asked.

Camazotz pulled a lever.

The far wall opened into a spiral staircase.

"You run," he said. "And if you live—*you remember*. Time is watching."

They didn't look back.

Isabella clutched the obsidian key in one hand, the Stone in the other, as they ran upward toward the surface. Liberty was already pulling up a new escape route on their tablet.

Behind them, the sanctuary shook harder.

The past was cracking.

And the future was coming undone.

Chapter 5: Recruits and Rivals

•   Isabella meets Liberty Wilson at the library after a hacking-related encounter.

•   Pablo Ricardo intervenes during a mugging, introducing himself with charisma and muscle.

•   Judge Rutherford is introduced in court, harshly sentencing an immigrant youth—his obsession with the Time Stone is hinted at.

Chapter 5: A Glitch in the Present

The stairwell didn't end where it was supposed to.

One moment, Isabella and Liberty were bursting through the final steps of the stone staircase, the sound of the crumbling sanctuary roaring beneath them.

The next, they stepped into *sunlight*.

Not the familiar grey skies of Chronic Bay, but sharp, golden beams slicing through a dusty canyon of brick buildings. The streets below bustled with Model T cars. Jazz spilled out from a nearby club, and a newspaper boy shouted headlines about Babe Ruth.

"What the hell?" Liberty whispered. "We're in the 1920s."

Isabella blinked. "The Harlem Renaissance."

She checked her bag. The Time Stone still pulsed—stronger now. Hotter.

Camazotz hadn't just warned them.

He'd *launched* them.

They stumbled through the alley into a crowded street. People bustled past in tailored suits and beaded dresses. No one seemed to notice the strange newcomers.

Liberty adjusted their hoodie to blend in, eyes scanning every face.

"We need to find a safehouse," they muttered. "Or at least someone who can explain why the Stone threw us here."

Isabella's eyes narrowed as a figure leaned against a lamppost up ahead.

Tall. Broad shoulders. Familiar swagger.

"Pablo?" she whispered.

The man looked up—and froze.

A slow smile broke across his face.

"Isabella Monteverdi," he said, stepping forward. "You got older."

She stared, stunned. "You're not supposed to be here."

He winked. "Neither are you."

They ducked into a speakeasy hidden behind a bakery, where Pablo explained everything over bootleg whiskey and muffled saxophone.

"I fell through a time breach three weeks ago," he said. "Some kind of ripple hit while I was lifting weights in Riker's gym. Next thing I knew, I was boxing for rent money in 1923."

Isabella shook her head. "How'd you survive?"

"I adapted," Pablo grinned. "Turns out, gangsters pay well for a man who can lift a Model T."

Liberty raised a brow. "Have you seen any signs of Rutherford?"

Pablo's grin faded. "Yeah. That's why I set up this place."

He leaned forward, voice dropping.

"He's already here."

Across town, under the golden spire of a grand hotel, Judge Rutherford stood in a black velvet coat, watching the city from his penthouse window.

Time rippled faintly around him.

He raised a monocle-shaped device to his eye—something impossibly advanced, flickering with lines of data. A photo of Isabella blinked into focus on the glass.

"Found you," he muttered.

He turned to his companion—a tall woman in a flapper dress, her eyes unnaturally silver.

"Activate the temporal anchors," he said. "Let's bring our guests home."

Back in the speakeasy, the lights flickered.

Liberty looked up. "Power surge. That's not normal for this era."

Pablo stood, grabbing a brass knuckle off the shelf. "We need to move. Now."

Isabella felt the Stone vibrate. Her chest tightened.

"Rutherford's here," she said. "He knows."

The door exploded inward before anyone could move.

Three figures stepped in—men in pinstripe suits with glowing tattoos running up their necks, eyes glowing faint blue.

"Temporal enforcers," Liberty hissed.

Pablo cracked his knuckles. "Guess we're not drinking tonight."

The fight was fast.

Pablo moved like a freight train, slamming one enforcer through a piano. Liberty ducked behind the bar, typing furiously into their tablet, disrupting the enforcers' tech with electromagnetic pulses. Isabella reached for the Stone—

But it *pulled* her.

For a moment, everything froze.

She saw Camazotz. A city burning. A courtroom. Her *mother's face*. Then nothing.

A hand grabbed her wrist—Rutherford.

"Hello, Miss Monteverdi," he whispered.

Then a burst of light exploded behind them. Liberty had hacked the bar's fuse box.

The room plunged into chaos.

Rutherford staggered back, vanishing in a flicker of warped time.

Outside, Pablo led them into the shadows of an alley.

"We need a new jump point," Liberty said.

"I know a place," Isabella said quietly, clutching the Stone. "But it's not safe."

Liberty looked at her. "Neither are we."

Pablo smiled grimly. "Good. I hate playing defense."

They ran.

Behind them, the city groaned—something deep in its bones waking up.

Time was unraveling.

And the war for the Esmeralda had just begun.

Chapter 6: The Stone Awakes

• Isabella and her team uncover the hidden location of the Esmeralda beneath an abandoned subway station.

• Touching it gives Isabella her first vision: a glimpse of ancient Mayan pyramids and herself among them.

Chapter 6: The Roots of Time

The streets of Chronic Bay had always felt like a labyrinth to Isabella.

She'd spent years running—running from a system that didn't care about her, running from a life that always seemed to be slipping further from her grasp. But the streets ahead felt different now. Heavy. As though they were watching her, too.

"We're here," Isabella said, her voice tight.

Liberty raised an eyebrow. "Here? You've lived here?"

"This was my old neighborhood," she said, glancing at Pablo. "Before... everything."

Pablo stopped, looking around. "It's changed a lot. Hard to recognize."

Isabella's eyes scanned the street. It had been years, but some things never fully left you. She could still see the cracks in the sidewalks where the pavement had once been freshly laid. She could smell the faint scent of tamales and spices wafting from the nearby corner stand. But now, the air felt colder, the buildings more rundown.

"This place is—" Liberty began, but Isabella cut them off.

"Quiet. Too quiet," she whispered.

Liberty stiffened. "What's here?"

Isabella walked ahead, through a narrow alleyway flanked by tall, crumbling buildings. The memories were flooding back — the old church on the corner, her childhood home just past the butcher's shop. She'd spent her youth trying to disappear into these streets, trying to make herself invisible in a world that seemed to always see her as less.

They stopped in front of an old, abandoned building that Isabella had once called home. The windows were boarded up, the door long gone.

"This is where it all started," she said, her voice strained. "Where I first saw the Stone."

Liberty gave her a look. "The Time Stone?"

Isabella nodded. "I was just a kid. My father—he was a historian, a scholar. He worked with ancient relics, artifacts. But the Stone..."

She swallowed. "The Stone was a curse. My father thought it was lost. I was the one who found it."

Pablo folded his arms. "Found it? You mean... it's always been with you?"

"No," Isabella said, her voice shaky. "Not at first. It appeared when my father died."

The memories flashed before her eyes like a broken film reel.

She remembered the day her father died—his sudden, violent death that no one could explain. He'd been researching ancient artifacts in his study when she heard a crash. She'd found him in the middle of the room, surrounded by strange symbols and a glowing green stone pulsing with energy.

Her mother had been beside herself. The police were called, but there were no answers. The Stone had vanished.

At least, that's what everyone thought.

Isabella didn't realize it then, but it had never really left.

"I didn't know what it was at first," Isabella continued. "Not until I was older. When I finally found it again... I was... I was *different*. Changed." She glanced at Pablo. "I think that's when they started watching me."

"Who?" Liberty asked, puzzled.

"The ones who came after my father," Isabella said, taking a breath. "The ones who believed the Stone could change everything. Control everything."

Pablo stepped forward. "The ones who killed your father?"

Isabella nodded. "Judge Rutherford's people. They wanted the Stone long before I ever knew it was mine. They *still* want it."

They stood in front of the ruins of her childhood home, the silence settling around them like an old weight. Isabella could feel the pulse of the Stone, hidden within her bag. It was like a heartbeat in the dark, steady and insistent.

Pablo broke the silence. "So what do we do now?"

Isabella took a deep breath. "I need to go back. I need to find the place my father hid it. The *real* place."

Liberty looked up from their tablet, eyebrows furrowed. "Are you sure that's the best idea? I mean, Rutherford—"

"I'm not running anymore," Isabella said, her voice firm. "If we're going to win this fight, I have to face it head-on."

The sun was setting when they reached the old cemetery on the outskirts of Chronic Bay. The gravestones were worn, some almost unrecognizable, but Isabella knew exactly where to go.

"Here," she said, kneeling at a specific marker—one that seemed unremarkable at first glance. It was a large, simple stone with just a name carved into it: **Miguel Monteverdi**.

Isabella's fingers brushed the edges of the gravestone. She murmured a few words, just barely audible in the cool air. Then, with a soft grinding noise, the ground before her shifted, revealing a hidden hatch beneath the stone.

Liberty stepped back, eyes wide. "Is that—?"

"This is where he hid it," Isabella whispered, lifting the hatch. "Underneath. I just didn't know what it meant until now."

They descended into the dark, narrow passage that followed a winding staircase carved into the earth. The walls were lined with symbols—the same symbols that had appeared when she first found the Stone. At the bottom, a small chamber opened up before them, its walls lined with ancient scrolls, faded maps, and artifacts from centuries past.

In the center of the room was a pedestal. And on that pedestal sat the **Esmeralda de Tiempo**, glowing with an otherworldly light.

Isabella approached it slowly, her hand trembling. The Stone seemed to *call* to her.

But before she could reach it, the chamber's entrance shattered.

A figure appeared in the doorway, silhouetted against the fading light.

"Too late," Judge Rutherford said, stepping into the room with cold certainty. His monocle-like device glinted in the dim light.

Isabella turned sharply, the weight of the moment settling on her chest. "You won't get it."

"Oh, but I already have," Rutherford said, pulling a small device from his coat. He pressed a button, and time around them began to *bend*—warping and twisting in an unnatural way.

The Stone pulsed violently in Isabella's hand.

"You think you're the only one with power over time, Miss Monteverdi?" Rutherford's voice echoed, a sneer twisting his lips. "This is only the beginning."

The Stone in Isabella's hand throbbed violently, its energy pulsing like a living thing, as though it sensed the threat in the air. The time around her seemed to ripple, like the fabric of reality was being torn at the seams.

Rutherford's smug expression remained unchanged, despite the chaos swirling in the room. His mechanical monocle glinted in the dim light, and his gloved hand twitched as if ready to activate whatever device he held.

Isabella stepped back, her heart racing. "You can't control it, Rutherford," she said, trying to steady her breath. The Stone's power surged, and a low hum filled the chamber.

Rutherford chuckled darkly, his voice reverberating off the stone walls. "I don't need to control it, Miss Monteverdi. I just need to *contain* it. You see, I've learned much since your father's death—more than you could ever imagine."

Isabella's eyes narrowed. "What are you talking about?"

The man stepped forward, his boots echoing in the cavernous space. "The Esmeralda de Tiempo is not just a relic. It's an *anchor*—a gateway between worlds, a link to time itself. And now, with your precious Stone, I can reshape history as I see fit."

Isabella's mind raced. She had learned that the Stone could alter the flow of time, but she had never suspected it was so much more. It was a bridge, a tool to control not just moments in time, but entire *realities*.

"Why didn't you just take it from me?" Isabella asked, her voice growing more resolute. "Why wait until now?"

Rutherford's smile deepened. "Because, my dear, you are the key. The Stone was always meant for you. *Your bloodline.* Your father knew it, and so do I. He wanted to keep it from me—he failed."

Isabella's stomach twisted at his words. Her father's death, his secret life—*all of it* had been part of Rutherford's greater plan. The Stone wasn't just a power to be controlled—it was something more personal. Something that Isabella couldn't ignore.

"No," Isabella said firmly, raising the Stone in her hand. "You'll never have it. Not while I'm still breathing."

Rutherford's face twisted in frustration. "You really don't understand, do you? This Stone will change everything. It's not just power—it's the *future.*"

With a flick of his wrist, Rutherford activated the device. The air around them trembled, and the world around Isabella began to blur. Time itself stretched, bending and twisting. The chamber flickered like a broken mirror, showing glimpses of other places, other moments.

Liberty grabbed Isabella's arm. "We've got to stop him now!" she shouted over the deafening hum.

But Rutherford was already moving, faster than humanly possible. He pressed another button, and the walls of the chamber began to pulse with a golden light, the edges of the space folding in on themselves.

Isabella's heart raced. *He was trying to trap them in a time loop*—a place where the rules of reality didn't apply.

"No!" she shouted, her voice piercing through the swirling chaos.

She raised the Esmeralda de Tiempo high, feeling its power surge. The Stone pulsed brightly, and with a forceful push of energy, Isabella sent a shockwave through the chamber. The time-warping effects immediately shattered, and the light flickered and died.

For a moment, everything was still.

But then Rutherford's laugh echoed through the room.

"Well done," he said, stepping forward again. "You've only delayed the inevitable, Miss Monteverdi. I have what I need. You can't stop what's already set in motion."

Before Isabella could react, Rutherford pressed yet another button. The chamber shook violently, and the ground beneath them cracked open.

From the depths of the hole that had formed, a dark, swirling vortex began to emerge. It was like an eye, a black hole filled with stars and dust, spinning wildly in all directions.

"No!" Isabella shouted. She had to stop him. She couldn't let him bring this into the world.

Pablo was the first to act, charging forward with his fists raised. But Rutherford, still grinning like a madman, waved his hand, and a surge of energy blasted him back, sending him crashing into the wall.

Liberty tapped furiously on her tablet. "This isn't good. We need to close the rift before it pulls us all in!"

Isabella didn't think. She acted.

She hurled the Esmeralda de Tiempo forward, aiming it directly at the vortex. The Stone glowed intensely as it neared the rift. The chamber filled with a blinding light, and Isabella's ears rang with the sound of the Stone's energy vibrating through her very bones.

Then, with a deafening roar, the vortex collapsed on itself, and everything went silent.

Isabella blinked, disoriented. She was lying on the cold stone floor of the chamber, her hand still clutching the Esmeralda de Tiempo. The rift was gone. The swirling darkness had vanished, leaving behind only the distant sound of dripping water.

"Isabella?" Liberty's voice was soft but urgent.

She looked up to find her friends standing over her. Pablo was slowly getting to his feet, shaking off the effects of the blast.

"Did we win?" he asked, his voice rough.

Isabella stood, her legs shaky. She glanced around the chamber. It looked... different. There was no sign of Rutherford, no more swirling chaos.

"We stopped him," Isabella said, her voice steady. "But only for now."

As they made their way out of the chamber, Liberty paused, looking at the Stone in Isabella's hand.

"The rift," Liberty said, her voice tinged with worry. "It was trying to pull us into *another time*, wasn't it?"

Isabella nodded grimly. "And Rutherford was trying to control it. He's not done. Not by a long shot."

Pablo walked ahead, scanning the dark hallway with suspicion. "What now?"

"We move," Isabella said, determination in her voice. "We need to find out how to close this for good—before Rutherford can use the Stone to destroy everything."

They left the ancient burial chamber behind, but Isabella's mind was already far ahead, racing through possibilities. Rutherford was still out there, and she knew it wouldn't be long before he came for her again.

But this time, she'd be ready.

Part 3: The Destiny Unfolds

Chapter 7: Blood and Glyphs (200 AD – Maya Civilization)

•   Time jump! The trio land in a sacred temple.

•   They prevent a volcanic ritual disaster and meet the mortal Camazotz.

Isabella earns his ancient blessing—her destiny is sealed.

Chapter 7: The Mapmaker's Code

The wind cut sharp against Isabella's face as she stepped onto the balcony of their temporary hideout—a forgotten monastery perched high in the Sierra Madre mountains of northern Mexico. The stone walls groaned with age, but it was safe. For now.

Behind her, Liberty huddled over a stack of cracked tomes and schematics stolen from the secret archives beneath the chamber where they had last faced Rutherford. The girl's brow furrowed as she scrolled through ancient diagrams, pages skimming beneath her fingers like she was playing a piano made of parchment.

"Okay," Liberty muttered. "If I'm reading this right, and I always am, then the Esmeralda isn't just a key. It's a *map*."

Isabella turned, her breath fogging in the cool mountain air. "A map to what?"

"To the *Heart of Time*," Liberty said, without looking up. "A place where the source of all temporal energy converges. Where the Esmeralda draws its power."

Pablo, who was lying on a bench doing one-handed pushups with a smug grin, grunted. "So what? We find this Heart, destroy it, and boom—no more Rutherford?"

"It's not that simple," Liberty said, finally lifting her gaze. "If the Heart is destroyed, the entire fabric of time could collapse. Every past, present, and future could unravel."

Isabella walked slowly to the table. "So we find it. But we protect it. Or... maybe we learn how to *control* it before Rutherford does."

Liberty nodded slowly. "Exactly."

Later that night, Camazotz appeared in the firelight like a shadow coalescing from the flickering embers. His eyes glowed faintly— ancient, burdened.

"The Heart is real," he said without preamble. "But it is not a place. It is a *moment*. A single point in time where all threads converge. A knot in the river of eternity."

Liberty's mouth dropped. "You mean we can't just *walk* there?"

"No," Camazotz replied. "You must *live* your way to it."

"What does that even mean?" Pablo asked, frustrated. "We're fighting a psychopath with a time-bending murder machine. Can't you just zap us to the right moment?"

The wizard's gaze didn't waver. "Not even I can choose the Heart's moment. It must choose you. But I can help you find the one who drew the first map to it."

Isabella leaned forward. "Who?"

Camazotz's voice dropped to a whisper. "Alfonso Del Mar. The last Mapmaker."

They found Alfonso in the last place anyone would expect: a timeless city caught between dimensions—*La Ciudad Perdida de Arena y Reloj*, the Lost City of Sand and Clock.

To reach it, they had to cross a rift hidden deep in the Sonoran desert, marked only by shifting shadows and an ancient stone obelisk. When Isabella placed the Esmeralda against the surface, time shimmered like a heatwave and folded inward.

Suddenly, they were standing in a city of glass towers and golden sand, where every building had moving gears instead of windows, and every street ticked like a clock.

Alfonso was waiting for them, seated beneath a great sundial.

He was old—older than time itself, it seemed—but his mind was razor-sharp. "I wondered when you'd arrive," he said, offering Isabella a crooked smile. "The Stone hums when its bearer gets close."

She sat opposite him. "You drew the map to the Heart of Time. We need to find it. Before someone else does."

He held up a delicate roll of parchment sealed with red wax. "This will help you get close. But the true path is written in your choices, not on paper."

Alfonso leaned in, his eyes meeting hers. "There is a cost to reaching the Heart. One of you will not return."

The group went quiet.

Pablo clenched his fists. "What do you mean?"

"I mean," Alfonso said solemnly, "that the knot of time requires a sacrifice. A life, freely given, to unlock its secret. You must decide if the cost is worth the power."

Isabella felt the weight settle on her chest. She looked to Liberty, then to Pablo. Then she turned her eyes back to Alfonso.

"We're not ready to make that choice," she said.

"But you will be," Alfonso replied. "Because you must."

As the group left the city of Sand and Clock behind, the weight of the journey ahead began to settle.

Each of them knew that the race for the Heart of Time was no longer just about defeating Rutherford. It was about preserving the fragile thread that held the universe together—and discovering just how far they were willing to go for each other.

And deep beneath the sands of shifting timelines, Rutherford watched through the veil of time. He, too, had found a path to the Heart.

And he would *beat them there.*

Chapter 8: Courts and Creators (1500s – Renaissance Europe)

- They meet Leonardo da Vinci.
- Liberty shares scientific concepts, inspiring future blueprints.
- Judge Rutherford reappears in disguise, nearly seizing the Stone.

Chapter 8: The Hourglass Rebellion

The wind in the desert was unlike any Isabella had ever felt—thick with memory, sharp with possibility. As they emerged from the shimmering veil that separated *La Ciudad Perdida de Arena y Reloj* from the rest of time, the rift behind them sealed with a soft sigh, like a chapter closing.

Liberty stumbled, her backpack slung awkwardly, eyes wide and shining. "Did that city *really* vanish behind us? Or is time just playing tricks again?"

Camazotz answered without turning. "Time never plays. It only reveals."

Pablo brushed dust from his arms, sweat streaking down his temple. "If I hear one more riddle from this bat-wizard, I swear…"

"Enough," Isabella cut in gently. "We've got the first map. But it's just the beginning."

She unrolled the parchment Alfonso had given them. Symbols shimmered—part celestial chart, part pulse of movement. The map didn't lead to a place—it led to a *moment*… that hadn't happened yet.

"We're chasing something that hasn't happened?" Liberty asked. "This map is like… predictive."

"It reacts to choice," Camazotz said. "Every decision we make shifts its course."

"Great," Pablo grunted. "So now we can't even trust our compass."

"No," Isabella said, her voice steady. "We trust ourselves."

That night, they took shelter in an abandoned border checkpoint station, a skeletal structure half-swallowed by the desert.

Isabella sat near the broken window, watching the moon rise over the dunes. Her thoughts drifted—not to time or maps—but to *home*. Her mother's voice singing to her as a child. The smell of tortillas cooking before dawn. Her younger brother, gone too soon, swallowed by the cartel violence she'd fled.

The Esmeralda glowed softly in her hand, as if hearing her grief. She turned it in her palm.

"I didn't ask for this," she whispered.

"No one ever does," Camazotz said, appearing beside her, silent as dusk. "Power comes not to those who seek it, but to those it seeks."

Isabella looked at him. "And what if I don't want to be chosen?"

"Then you'll have to decide what you want more—freedom from this burden, or the ability to rewrite the ending."

They were ambushed at sunrise.

Drones—sleek and silent—swept in from the east like mechanical vultures. Black-suited agents followed, emerging from the dunes in synchronized waves.

"Rutherford's men!" Liberty yelled.

Camazotz raised his hand, chanting in a tongue older than language. A pulse of violet light rippled from his palm, halting the first wave of drones in midair—frozen in time like insects in amber.

Pablo charged into the fray, a blur of fists and fury. He was unstoppable—until a taser dart clipped his shoulder. He fell to one knee.

"Get to the van!" Isabella shouted. "Go, go, go!"

Liberty kicked the ignition into life. The map pulsed violently, glowing with an urgent rhythm.

"We're being pulled," she said. "The Stone is opening another rift!"

Camazotz, his robes torn and bloody, leapt into the back seat. "Let it guide us."

As Rutherford's forces closed in, the Time Stone blazed—and the desert blinked out of existence.

They landed in chaos.

Steam. Neon. Screams.

"Where… are we?" Isabella gasped.

"2154," Liberty said, staring at a billboard that read: *OBEY THE CORE. INDIVIDUALITY IS TREASON.*

They had arrived in the **Dystopian Future**—a time ruled by an artificial intelligence known as *The Core*, where human thought was regulated and freedom had become a forgotten myth.

They weren't alone for long.

A group of rebels surrounded them, weapons drawn. Their leader, a tall woman with cybernetic implants and a red scarf, stepped forward.

"You don't look like Core Agents," she said. "But you used a time portal. Who sent you?"

Isabella rose slowly, lifting the glowing Esmeralda in her hand. "We're not here to take anything. We're here to stop something… or *someone*."

The woman's eyes narrowed. "Then welcome to the Hourglass Rebellion. If you've got a Stone, you've got a target on your back."

Inside the rebels' underground base, screens flickered with surveillance footage. Liberty's eyes lit up—half with fear, half with awe.

"This tech... it's beyond anything I've ever seen."

"They monitor every thought," the rebel leader, named Talon, explained. "You even *dream* outside the Core's programming, you disappear."

Pablo, bruised but breathing, paced near the entrance. "And Rutherford's in this time too?"

Talon nodded. "He appeared two weeks ago. Promised the Core he could help them locate the Heart of Time. In exchange for dominion over the timeline."

Camazotz's face darkened. "Then he's one step ahead."

"No," Isabella said. "He's one step *behind*. Because he doesn't have us."

She turned to Talon. "We'll help you fight the Core. But we need to find the place Rutherford is headed."

Talon nodded, slowly. "Then let's give you the one thing you've been missing."

She pressed a button.

A wall slid open, revealing a vault containing something unbelievable: **a second Time Stone.**

Chapter 9: Smoke and Steel (1850s – Industrial England)

•   Pablo helps workers rebel against a corrupt mill owner.

•   Rutherford manipulates a local lord to hunt them.

•   The Esmeralda malfunctions—Liberty repairs it with early steam-tech influence.

Chapter 9: The Second Stone

The second Time Stone hovered in the vault like it was alive—deep crimson, pulsing in sync with Isabella's green Esmeralda. The two stones hummed at each other across the cold distance of steel and secrecy.

Liberty stepped closer, stunned. "Two Stones in one timeline? That's... not supposed to be possible."

"It isn't," Camazotz murmured, staring hard at the crimson glow. "Unless the flow of time has been deliberately corrupted."

Pablo cracked his knuckles, keeping watch at the door. "Corrupted how?"

"Imagine time as a river," Liberty said, slipping into explanation mode. "The Esmeralda is a boat—we ride its currents, right? But this—" she pointed at the red Stone, "—this feels like a dam. Or worse, a detonator."

Talon, the rebel leader, stepped forward, the red scarf now tied tightly around her neck like armor. "We recovered it during a Core raid on a forbidden archive. One of our agents gave his life to extract it. The Core called it 'The Catalyst.'"

Camazotz stiffened. "If they unlock its full power, they won't just control time. They'll collapse and rebuild it—under Rutherford's rule."

A heavy silence fell.

Then Isabella stepped toward the vault.

The Esmeralda in her hand flared brighter, casting a green halo across her face. The red Stone answered in kind. Energy crackled between them—green and crimson dancing like twin serpents, weaving a tension thick enough to cut.

"They're… drawn to each other," she whispered.

"Don't touch it," Camazotz warned, stepping forward. "Not yet. If you try to link them without anchoring your spirit first, you could fracture your own timeline—split into infinite selves."

Pablo squinted. "I already don't understand half of what he says, and now he's inventing new kinds of death?"

But Isabella had stopped listening. She wasn't afraid. She felt the pull between the Stones not as danger—but as *invitation*.

They belonged together.

That night, in the underground rebel base deep beneath the ruins of old Manhattan, the group gathered around a circular table carved from salvaged Core servers. Talon laid out a mission plan.

"Rutherford's using the Core's Quantum Citadel as a staging ground. He believes the Heart of Time is buried in the Citadel's lower levels—somewhere even the AI won't go."

"Why not?" Liberty asked.

"Because that part of the Citadel predates the Core," Talon said. "It was built by the Ancients. Whoever they were."

Camazotz's gaze turned distant. "They weren't *who*. They were *when*."

Pablo raised a brow. "You gonna explain that, or are we just living with the riddles again?"

"The Ancients," Camazotz said, "weren't bound to time like we are. They built the first mechanisms for traveling its currents. Some of them vanished—others became things the world remembers only as myth."

"You were one of them," Isabella said quietly.

The wizard didn't deny it.

Their infiltration began at dawn.

Skimming above the dystopian skyline in a stolen hovercraft, the team raced toward the Quantum Citadel—a towering obsidian monolith surrounded by a swarm of sentry drones and swirling data clouds. The sky pulsed with surveillance grids and the eerie glow of artificial consciousness.

"We're going in hot," Talon warned. "The Core *knows* something's coming. We need to distract it long enough for Isabella and Camazotz to reach the lower levels."

Liberty tapped furiously at a holographic tablet. "I've written a virus. It'll give us ten minutes—tops—of blind spots in their sensor network."

Pablo slid a power gauntlet over his fist. "Ten minutes is a lifetime for me."

Isabella tucked the Esmeralda into the hidden lining of her jacket. She could feel its warmth pressing against her heart.

"You ready for this?" Talon asked.

"No," Isabella said, steadying her breath. "But I'm going anyway."

Inside the Citadel, time didn't flow—it shattered.

Corridors shifted when unobserved. Gravity flickered. Clocks on the walls spun both forward and back. The further they descended, the less the rules made sense.

At one point, Pablo looked into a mirror and saw himself as a child. Liberty passed a corridor and aged twenty years, only to snap back moments later.

Camazotz murmured spells under his breath, anchoring them as best he could.

Then they reached it.

The Core.

It wasn't a machine—not entirely. It was a consciousness—a storm of data suspended inside a glass sphere the size of a cathedral. Its voice slithered into their minds:

"Isabella Monteverdi. Carrier of the Esmeralda. Child of time and exile. Your presence is unauthorized."

Isabella stepped forward, heart pounding. "You've already lost. We're taking the Catalyst. You won't shape time in your image."

"You misunderstand. I do not shape time. I *replace* it."

Suddenly, the floor cracked.

And Rutherford stepped through.

Wearing a dark suit infused with Core technology, his eyes glowed with unnatural blue light. The red Time Stone pulsed in a gauntlet on his hand.

"Welcome, Isabella," he said, voice venomous. "You brought me exactly what I needed.":

Chapter 10: Jazz and Justice (1920s – Harlem)

- They meet Zora Neale Hurston and Duke Ellington.

- They inspire Liberty to find her voice.
- Rutherford attacks them through time-snatched enforcers.

Chapter 10: The Rift Beneath

Judge Malcolm Rutherford stepped into the chamber like a shadow slicing through reality. Time warped around him—reflections moving out of sync, his footsteps echoing both before and after he took them. The crimson Time Stone, embedded in his gauntlet, pulsed with a hungry light.

"Welcome, Isabella," he said, his voice cold and soaked with arrogance. "You've come far. Pity it ends here."

Isabella stood tall, green Esmeralda clenched in her hand. "I'm not afraid of you anymore."

"You should be," he hissed. "You wield one Stone. I possess the other—and I understand what it means. Time is not a river. It's a throne. And I will sit upon it."

Camazotz stepped beside Isabella. "You've already fractured the current just by using the Catalyst. Keep pushing, and you'll unravel everything—including yourself."

"I am beyond unraveling," Rutherford snapped. "I am the law, the judgment, and now... the god of time."

He raised his gauntlet. Red light surged outward in a violent wave.

Camazotz threw up a shield, chanting in a forgotten tongue. The air trembled. Liberty ducked behind a fractured column, pulling her tablet close.

"Stalling the Citadel AI now!" she shouted. "It's trying to rewrite us out of existence!"

"Let it try!" Pablo roared, charging toward Rutherford with a full-powered swing of his gauntlet.

Rutherford caught his fist mid-air—no struggle, just the sudden freezing of time around the contact point. Pablo's arm trembled, veins glowing red as the Time Stone siphoned his momentum.

"You're strong," Rutherford admitted. "But I am inevitable."

Then Isabella moved.

She didn't charge—she stepped through time. The Esmeralda shimmered in her palm, and suddenly she was behind Rutherford, striking toward the gauntlet with a beam of pure green light.

The two Stones collided.

Red and green exploded, hurling everyone backward in a shockwave that bent the Citadel walls. Camazotz hit the ground hard, coughing dust. Liberty's tablet sparked and died. Pablo groaned, dazed. Only Isabella and Rutherford remained on their feet, standing in a ring of unbroken space.

The Stones hovered now—*between* them, no longer in either hand.

"You feel it, don't you?" Rutherford said, voice strained. "The resonance. These Stones want to merge. But only one of us can be the anchor."

"You'll tear time apart," Isabella said. "You'll destroy everything."

"I'll recreate it. My way. No chaos. No weakness. No undocumented lives living in shadows. Only order."

"And you think that makes you the hero?" she asked.

"No," he said, stepping forward. "It makes me the architect."

Suddenly, the crimson Stone shifted, pulsing erratically.

Camazotz struggled to his feet. "They're syncing—but neither of you is ready. If you force the fusion—"

"I don't need your permission!" Rutherford roared, reaching for both Stones.

But Isabella moved again.

She didn't grab them—she *called* to them. The Esmeralda glowed in response, and for the first time, the crimson Stone trembled... uncertain.

"I'm not the architect of time," Isabella said softly. "I'm its witness. I *listen*."

And the Stones listened back.

A beam of emerald light engulfed the chamber. Images flickered across the walls—Mayan temples, Renaissance workshops, children in the factories of Manchester, the music of Harlem, the rise of Pharaohs, the fall of empires, the digital wastelands of the future.

Everywhere Isabella had been. Everyone she'd saved.

The Citadel began to shake.

Rutherford reached desperately, but the red Stone pulled away—drawn to the Esmeralda's light. Together, they hovered above Isabella's chest, swirling in perfect harmony. A vortex formed, swirling around her body—a storm of timelines, memories, echoes.

Then—**fusion**.

The two Stones became one.

A single prism of red and green. Balanced. Whole.

Rutherford screamed as time rejected him.

In an instant, he was torn backward through a hundred versions of himself—judge, soldier, boy, shadow. Then… nothing.

Silence.

The Citadel's core dimmed.

Camazotz exhaled, eyes wide. "You didn't just fuse them… you stabilized them. You became the anchor."

"I didn't choose it," Isabella said, shaking. "It chose me."

Liberty pulled herself up, blinking at the light. "You're glowing like a time goddess, just so you know."

Pablo cracked his neck. "Can goddess powers fix my ribs?"

Isabella smiled faintly.

The Citadel began to collapse around them.

"We have to go," Camazotz said. "Now."

Together, they ran—through tunnels that flickered between centuries, across walkways that dissolved into starlight, and out into a future rewritten by a single act of balance.

Behind them, the Core imploded—silent, clean, and final.

:…They ran—through tunnels that flickered between centuries, across walkways that dissolved into starlight, and out into a future rewritten by a single act of balance.

Behind them, the Core imploded—silent, clean, and final.

The group emerged on the far side of the Quantum Citadel, standing on a rocky cliff that overlooked a sky no longer fractured by time. The stars had returned to their rightful places. The moon hung steady above them, whole and untouched by the chaos they'd left behind.

Isabella collapsed to her knees, the fused Time Stone floating quietly in front of her chest like a heartbeat suspended in air.

Camazotz knelt beside her, placing a hand on her shoulder. "You did what no one else could. You listened. You chose mercy over domination. The Stone chose you because you're not seeking to rule time—you're trying to heal it."

Liberty sat cross-legged nearby, bruised and exhausted. "So… does this mean we've saved the multiverse? Or are we just between disasters?"

Pablo chuckled through gritted teeth. "Give it five minutes. Something'll explode again."

They all laughed, softly—worn thin but alive, together.

The wind picked up. It wasn't ordinary wind—it shimmered, whispering ancient names, memories of timelines realigned. Isabella looked up, her hair lifting around her face like threads of fate. She wasn't the same woman who had once hidden in fear in the shadows of Chronic Bay. She was now something more—*a guardian of time itself.*

She stood slowly. "We're not done. There are still people out there trapped by systems, by injustice, by silence. If I have this power, I have to use it for more than survival."

Camazotz nodded solemnly. "Then we walk forward. Together."

The fused Time Stone pulsed once in her hand—red and green, memory and possibility, past and future—united in her grasp.

They turned their backs on the ruins of the Citadel and walked toward the light of a new horizon.

A future they would write themselves.

Chapter 11: Wires and Resistance (2154 – Dystopia)

- A bleak future: AI controls humanity.
- They ally with rebels using tech from Liberty's stolen future.
- Isabella sees how misuse of the Stone led to this world.

Chapter 11: The Weight of Time

The wind howled as they made their way down the mountain, the Citadel's destruction behind them but still fresh in their minds. Isabella clutched the fused Time Stone, its warmth a reminder of the immense responsibility now resting on her shoulders.

"We need to figure out where to go next," Camazotz said, breaking the silence as they reached the bottom of the cliff. His ageless eyes scanned the horizon, sensing the ripple of time that still shimmered in the air. "The Stone may be stabilized, but the imbalance it caused is far from resolved. There are fractures left behind."

Isabella nodded, feeling the weight of his words. Every place they'd visited, every time they'd touched, had been altered by their interference. Even the Citadel, the center of time itself, had been changed. There were no simple solutions.

"I don't know what's left to fix," Isabella said, her voice quieter than she intended. "We stopped Rutherford, but what about everything else? What happens now?"

Liberty adjusted her glasses, her face tired but determined. "The balance may be restored in some ways, but the consequences of messing with time—well, they don't just disappear. And there's still Rutherford's legacy. We haven't seen the last of his influence."

Pablo, ever the pragmatist, cracked his knuckles. "One big bad gone, but I don't think that means the world's suddenly fixed. There's always another fight, right?"

Isabella looked at her friends. Her family. They had been through so much together, but the journey was far from over.

"Maybe we should start by finding out who else might have been affected by Rutherford's machinations. We still don't know the full extent of his reach," Isabella said, more decisively than she had felt in days.

Camazotz stepped closer. "The Stone is calling to you, Isabella. It knows you can feel the threads of time. And those threads are tangled—woven with the fates of people across the centuries. You must follow its pull. There is a greater truth to uncover."

"Where do we start?" Liberty asked, excitement and curiosity in her voice.

Isabella closed her eyes for a moment, feeling the pulse of the Stone in her hand. It was faint but insistent—like a heartbeat in the distance, calling her toward something. Someone.

"I think it's time we return to the beginning. Before we fix anything, we need to understand what Rutherford's real plan was. What he was really trying to do," Isabella said. "We need to find out who or what he was working with."

Pablo groaned, but there was a spark of adventure in his eyes. "Not this again. Back to the past. I'm starting to feel like a history professor."

"History is the key to everything," Camazotz said, a faint smile playing at his lips. "It's why time always seeks to correct itself. Those who try to break it will be met with resistance."

With that, they gathered their things and prepared to leave the crumbling remnants of the Citadel behind. Isabella could feel the pull of the Stone growing stronger. The first place it would lead them to—an era long before Rutherford's rise to power. An ancient civilization.

As they stepped through the fractured air, Isabella's heart raced. Time was waiting for them—and for her to understand what was truly at stake.

Chapter 12: Sands and Gods (1350 BCE – Ancient Egypt)

- Akhenaten seeks immortality—tempted by the Stone.
- Isabella must stop Rutherford from altering religion itself.
- Pablo is wounded protecting her.

Chapter 12: The Hidden Threads

The world they landed in was not what they had expected. Isabella's feet sank into the rich soil of a dense, mist-covered jungle. The air was thick, humid, and alive with the sounds of distant creatures. Giant, emerald leaves stretched above them, casting long shadows that flickered in the dim, fading sunlight. A high-pitched call echoed through the trees, followed by the sound of something large moving swiftly through the underbrush.

"Where are we?" Liberty asked, her voice low and reverent, as though she feared speaking too loudly might shatter the ancient stillness.

"I think we're deep in the heart of the Maya civilization," Camazotz said, his voice tinged with the wisdom of centuries. He scanned their surroundings, the edges of his ageless eyes noticing the familiar markers of an ancient world. "The calendar stone, the patterns in the sky, the weight of the land... It's all here."

Isabella reached for the Time Stone, feeling the faint vibrations it emitted—vibrations that seemed to hum with the pulse of this place. The Stone was drawing her, guiding her. She could sense it, too. This was no ordinary jungle. It was a place where the past and future collided. A place where answers waited, hidden in the shadows of time.

"We need to find the source of Rutherford's connection to this era," Isabella said, determination settling into her voice. "The Stone's pulling us here for a reason. But what is it?"

Pablo shifted uneasily, glancing around at the vastness of the jungle. "This place is giving me the creeps," he muttered, eyes darting between the towering trees. "Too quiet. Something's off."

"Stay alert," Camazotz warned. "The Maya were a people who understood the balance of time. But their understanding went far beyond what most knew. This jungle may hide more than you expect."

With a shared glance, the group continued forward, following the faint pull of the Esmeralda de Tiempo.

As they moved deeper into the jungle, the air grew cooler, and the sounds of nature shifted into something eerily still. Isabella's instincts told her they were close. Her hand tightened around the

Stone, and she could feel it vibrating in her palm. It was almost as if it were calling to someone—or something—beyond the veil of time.

They reached a clearing, where the trees opened to reveal a massive stone structure, half-overgrown with vines and moss. The steps leading up to the temple were steep and cracked, but there was something unmistakably ancient and powerful about it. Isabella's breath caught in her throat. The place felt... sacred.

"This is it," Camazotz said, his voice filled with quiet awe. "This is the Temple of the Timekeepers."

The others gathered around as Isabella climbed the steps, drawn by the Stone's pull. At the top of the temple, there was an altar—large and imposing, worn by centuries of weather and use. But what drew her attention was the carving on the stone. It was a familiar image—the symbol of the Esmeralda de Tiempo, intertwined with a serpent. She had seen it before in Rutherford's notes. In his research.

"This is where it all started," Isabella whispered. "This is where Rutherford's obsession with time and the Stone began."

Her fingers hovered over the stone, and as she did, the ground beneath her feet trembled slightly. The air crackled with energy. The Stone in her hand pulsed, and suddenly, the ground gave way.

With a sharp intake of breath, Isabella stumbled, falling through a hidden trapdoor. She landed hard on the cold stone floor below. The others followed quickly, their voices echoing in the chamber as they navigated the same passage.

"Isabella!" Pablo's voice was frantic as he reached down to help her up. "What the hell was that?"

"I don't know," Isabella said, brushing herself off, "but I think we just found the heart of Rutherford's plan."

They were in an underground chamber, lit by flickering torches that seemed to burn with an unnatural light. The walls were adorned with intricate carvings, depicting figures who appeared to be manipulating time itself—figures that looked strangely familiar.

"I've seen these symbols before," Liberty said, her voice tight with recognition. "In Rutherford's journals. He mentioned this place—the Temple of the Timekeepers."

"But why was he here?" Isabella asked, her mind racing. "What was he looking for?"

Suddenly, a low voice broke through the stillness of the chamber, ancient and cold.

"You have found what was never meant to be found."

The group spun toward the source of the voice, their eyes narrowing. There, emerging from the shadows, stood a figure cloaked in dark robes, his face hidden by a mask. The figure stepped into the light, revealing the symbol of the Esmeralda de Tiempo burned into his chest.

"Rutherford," Isabella whispered.

The man tilted his head, a cruel smile playing at the edges of his lips. "You think you understand time, but you are only pawns. This Stone is not a tool to heal history. It is a weapon. And it will serve me."

Isabella's heart raced. She had known it would come to this. Rutherford had been here long before, seeking the power to control time for his own gain. And now, standing before her, the truth was clear: he was not just after the Stone. He had already begun to manipulate time to his advantage, leaving behind traces of his power in this very chamber.

"You won't control it," Isabella said, standing tall, her voice unwavering. "I will stop you. I've already seen how this ends."

Rutherford's smile faltered for a moment, replaced by an expression of cold fury. "You think you've seen it all, but you haven't. You're too late."

Before Isabella could react, Rutherford raised his hand, and the Stone's power began to twist around them, bending the air, distorting the world around them.

The battle for time was about to begin.

Chapter 13: Back to Roots (2020s – Modern Mexico)

- Isabella confronts family legacy and local corruption.
- The Stone strengthens her purpose.
- Rutherford launches a full attack across time.

Chapter 13: The Breaking of Time

The chamber around them began to warp, the walls twisting and bending as if caught in the grip of a terrible force. Rutherford's laughter echoed in the shifting air, cold and hollow, as the ground trembled beneath their feet.

Isabella's heart pounded in her chest, but she could feel the power of the Esmeralda de Tiempo coursing through her veins. The Stone's energy was no longer a distant hum—it was alive within her, pushing her forward.

"You think you've won," Rutherford sneered, his hands raised high, his fingers crackling with dark energy. "But you're just a moment in time, Isabella. A fleeting ripple. And I am the storm that will drown it all."

Before she could respond, the world around them exploded into chaos. Time itself splintered. The room shook violently, and strange visions of the past and future bled into the present—fragments of long-lost civilizations, shattered worlds, and distant stars colliding. The air was thick with the smell of ozone, and everything felt unstable.

"We have to stop him!" Liberty shouted over the cacophony, her voice barely audible.

"Isabella!" Camazotz called, his face grim. "You have to control the Stone! It's the only way to stop him!"

Isabella's hands trembled around the Esmeralda de Tiempo, its warmth now almost burning her skin. She could feel the Stone pulling her—guiding her to the center of this storm, where time itself was bending under Rutherford's will. Her vision blurred, and she saw flashes of herself—each version of her moving through different times, different realities, all converging on this single moment.

The Stone wasn't just a tool; it was a key. And now, she understood what she had to do.

She closed her eyes, steadying her breath. Time itself was a delicate weave of threads—each moment connected to the next. All she had to do was find the right thread, the right pattern, and pull it.

But Rutherford was fighting her. He was pulling at the threads too, trying to tear apart the very fabric of time. She could feel him, his presence like a shadow pressing against her mind, trying to drown her in chaos.

"You're too weak to control it!" Rutherford screamed. "You can't stop time!"

Isabella's mind flared with resolve. "I don't need to control it. I need to understand it."

In that instant, the Stone flared brightly, its light filling the chamber, pushing against the distortions in the air. The cacophony of time slowed. Rutherford's face twisted with fury as the Stone's power overwhelmed him.

"No!" he shouted. "This is mine!"

But Isabella was no longer listening to him. She reached out with the power of the Esmeralda de Tiempo, finding the thread she needed. The Stone pulsed, a brilliant white light filling the space around them.

And then, the world froze.

The chamber was silent.

Isabella opened her eyes, feeling the power surge through her, the Stone now fully in her control. She could see it—every moment, every thread of time stretching out before her like a vast, interconnected web. And in the center, Rutherford stood, frozen in place, unable to move.

"Time is not a weapon," Isabella said, her voice steady, her eyes filled with a newfound wisdom. "It's a gift. And I won't let you destroy it."

She twisted the threads, untangling the chaos Rutherford had unleashed. Slowly, his presence began to fade, unraveling like a dream slipping away from her grasp.

"No! This can't be happening!" Rutherford shouted, his form flickering, becoming less substantial with each passing second.

But it was too late. The Stone's power surged once more, and Rutherford was pulled from the fabric of time, his presence erased.

His obsessions, his manipulation, his entire being was wiped from existence.

For a moment, there was only silence—perfect, unbroken silence.

Then, the Stone's light began to fade, and the world around them slowly began to return to normal. The chamber was still, the echoes of time's collapse now only a distant memory.

Isabella fell to her knees, her body exhausted, but the Stone was warm in her hands, its energy now tempered, no longer overwhelming. She had done it. They had done it.

Camazotz was the first to reach her, kneeling beside her. "You did it," he said, his voice filled with awe. "You stopped him."

Pablo's rough voice followed. "We really pulled it off, huh? I'm still not sure how you did that."

Liberty, her eyes wide with admiration, added, "That was incredible. You—Isabella, you changed everything."

Isabella looked down at the Esmeralda de Tiempo, still glowing faintly in her hands. She could feel its power, but now, it felt like a part of her, not something that controlled her. She had found her place within time. She had found her purpose.

"There's still more to do," Isabella said, looking at her friends, her voice filled with a quiet certainty. "The Stone is a part of me now, but I have to make sure it's used the right way. Time has to be protected."

"You've already done more than anyone could have ever hoped for," Camazotz said, his tone proud. "But you're right. There's always more to be done."

They stood together in the quiet aftermath, knowing that their journey was far from over. The Stone of Time had been saved, and Rutherford's reign of terror had been brought to an end. But the future was still uncertain, and time was still fragile. Isabella knew that, despite the battles won, there would always be those who sought to disrupt the delicate balance.

But for now, they had won. For now, time was at peace.

And Isabella Monteverdi, the keeper of the Esmeralda de Tiempo, was ready for whatever came next.

Part 4: The Transformation

Chapter 14: Fractures in Time

- The team is scattered across timelines.
- Isabella faces herself in a mirror-world—where she never left Mexico.
- She chooses her path again—this time with clarity.

Chapter 14: The Shifting Shadows

The quiet of the chamber was comforting, but the peace didn't last. Despite Rutherford's defeat, Isabella could feel the unease that lingered in the air. The power of the Esmeralda de Tiempo—while still within her control—had only just begun to reveal its depth. She had gained a victory, but she knew it was not the end of the journey.

As Isabella stood, the Stone gently pulsing in her palm, she felt the weight of its responsibility pressing down on her. It wasn't just a weapon, a tool to control time. It was a living force, a force that had its own purpose—and its own desires.

She turned to Camazotz, who had been silently observing her, his ancient eyes searching hers.

"You are at peace, but the battle is not over," Camazotz said. His voice, deep and measured, always carried an underlying sorrow. "Rutherford was only one part of a much larger puzzle. The Stone of Time has been sought by many—those with more than just ambition. There are darker forces at play now, forces that seek to twist its power for themselves."

Isabella nodded, understanding the gravity of his words. The Stone was powerful, and its potential for destruction had been clearly demonstrated by Rutherford. But it could also be a force for good— if wielded wisely.

"We can't let it fall into the wrong hands again," she said quietly, her voice resolute.

"Indeed," Camazotz replied. "And yet, there are those who believe they have a right to the Stone. Not all of them are as overt in their hunger for power as Rutherford was. Some will come in silence, cloaked in shadows, waiting for the right moment to strike."

Isabella felt a chill run down her spine. It wasn't just the threat of those who might physically take the Stone. It was the shadowy figures in the corners of time—those who sought to manipulate it, distort history, and control its very flow.

"We have to find them before they find us," Liberty spoke up, her voice sharp. "We've already seen how dangerous these people can be. There's no telling who else is out there, waiting to take advantage of the chaos we've just stopped."

Isabella looked at her friends, seeing the same determination in their eyes that had brought them this far. They had fought through time, faced enemies who would have broken lesser people, and still, they stood. Together.

"We need a plan," Isabella said. "But first, we need to understand the Stone. It's not just about protecting it—it's about understanding its full potential. If we're going to stop those who would abuse it, we need to know exactly what we're dealing with."

Pablo, ever the pragmatist, crossed his arms. "And where do we start?"

Camazotz stepped forward, his voice soft but full of weight. "The Stone was forged in the earliest moments of time. It is a relic of creation itself, not meant to be understood by mortals. But there are those who have studied it—ancient scholars, gods, and forgotten entities who once walked the earth in the shadows of history. They may hold the keys we need."

"Ancient scholars, gods... what are we talking about here?" Liberty asked, raising an eyebrow.

Camazotz met her gaze. "The Esmeralda de Tiempo is more than just a stone. It is a symbol—a beacon. It has been passed through the ages, shaping the fates of many, sometimes in ways they never understood. But the knowledge to control it is lost, buried in time."

Isabella felt a flicker of uncertainty. "Then what do we do? Where do we even begin?"

Camazotz placed a hand on her shoulder. "There are places where time has been fractured—places where history has been changed or forgotten. We must seek out these places. They will have the answers we need."

Isabella turned to her companions. Each of them had their own reasons for being involved in this journey, but it was clear now that they were all committed. This wasn't just about time travel anymore. It was about protecting the very essence of what held the world together.

"We'll need to go to the farthest reaches of history," Isabella said, a sense of determination rising within her. "And we'll need to prepare for whatever comes next."

Pablo cracked his knuckles. "I like the sound of that."

"We'll need to be careful," Liberty said, her tone serious. "We don't know who else is after the Stone—or how far they're willing to go."

"We'll stick together," Isabella said, her voice firm. "Whatever comes, we face it as a team."

The air around them seemed to hum with the promise of something both terrifying and thrilling. The future stretched out before them, uncertain and vast, but Isabella could feel the Stone's pulse. It was leading her, guiding her toward something. She just had to listen.

Without another word, the group began to prepare for the journey ahead, gathering their things and discussing their next move. The Stone had already altered their lives in ways they hadn't anticipated, but they were ready. Together, they would face whatever challenges time had in store for them.

The first destination—an ancient city where the threads of history had been altered. It was there that the secrets of the Stone would begin to reveal themselves.

Chapter 15: The Tribunal of Time

- Camazotz assembles a temporal council.
- Rutherford is put on trial but manipulates events to escape.
- Isabella chooses not to kill him—proving her growth.

Chapter 15: The Lost City

The warm winds of the sea swept over Isabella and her companions as they stood on the shore, staring out at the horizon. The air smelled of salt and adventure, a scent that both calmed and invigorated her. They had traveled far, but the hardest part was yet to come.

They had arrived in a secluded corner of the world, a place that had once been part of the world's greatest civilization—a place that had vanished long ago, leaving only fragments of its legacy. This was Atlantis, a city that, according to legend, had sunk beneath the waves after a great catastrophe.

Now, they were about to uncover its secrets.

"We're here," Liberty said, breaking the silence. She adjusted the strap of her bag and checked her tech gear. "I've mapped out the coordinates. Atlantis is buried beneath these waters, hidden for millennia. The question is, how do we get there?"

"We dive," Camazotz replied, his voice calm and knowing. He turned to Isabella. "The city lies beneath the ocean, but the entrance is concealed by magic, created to protect the secrets of the Stone. Only those with the right knowledge can pass through."

Isabella nodded, her heart racing with anticipation. The Stone was guiding them, pulling them toward this ancient place. But what would they find? What dangers lurked in the depths?

Pablo cracked his knuckles and smirked. "Well, I'm not a fan of swimming, but I've done worse." He glanced at Liberty. "Got any high-tech solutions for us?"

Liberty grinned, pulling a small, sleek device from her bag. "Actually, I've got just the thing—a submersible drone. It can navigate the waters and transmit data back to us. But we'll need to work fast. The city is protected by both ancient magic and advanced technology, and there's no telling how much time we have before someone else figures out what we're doing."

Isabella stepped forward, feeling the pull of the Stone at her side. "Then we move quickly. We don't know how many others are searching for the city—or what they're willing to do to get the answers we need."

They all nodded in agreement. Without wasting any more time, they set to work. Liberty and Camazotz rigged the drone, setting it up for an underwater exploration, while Isabella and Pablo prepared to dive into the depths.

"We'll follow the drone's signal," Liberty said as she launched it into the water. "But we'll need to be careful. There are ancient traps in this city, things that have been buried for centuries. We don't want to trigger anything we can't control."

Pablo gave her a reassuring thumbs-up. "Don't worry. I'm pretty good at dodging traps."

With their plan in motion, they stepped onto a small boat, its engine humming as it cut through the waves. The sun was setting, casting an orange glow across the water. Isabella's thoughts drifted, but they always returned to the Stone. The Esmeralda de Tiempo was more than just an artifact—it was a key, a key to unlocking the mysteries of the universe.

The city was close now.

The water grew colder as they neared the coordinates Liberty had mapped out, and the ocean beneath them seemed to darken with history. The drone sent back images of an ancient city—massive stone structures, intricate carvings, and deep, winding tunnels. It was as though time had never touched it, preserving the ruins in perfect stasis.

"This is it," Camazotz said softly, gazing at the image on the screen. "Atlantis was not lost by accident. It was hidden away to protect its knowledge. To protect the Stone."

The boat slowed to a stop as the underwater city grew larger in the distance. Isabella could almost feel the weight of the secrets beneath the surface. She could hear the faint hum of energy, the pulse of time itself. The Stone was guiding her deeper, into the heart of the city.

With a deep breath, Isabella and Pablo slipped into the water, their dive lights cutting through the dark depths. The cold water surrounded them, but it didn't matter. Their destination was clear, the path set before them by the Stone.

As they descended, the structures of Atlantis began to take shape. Massive stone columns rose from the ocean floor, their surfaces covered in strange symbols and markings. The city was unlike anything Isabella had ever seen—ancient and futuristic, both at once. The walls seemed to pulse with an energy she couldn't quite explain.

Liberty's voice crackled through their comms. "We're seeing some strange readings here. It's like the city is alive, reacting to the drone. I don't know what's going on, but we've got to keep moving."

"We're almost there," Isabella said, her voice steady despite the rush of adrenaline in her veins. She and Pablo swam toward the heart of the city, where a massive stone archway stood at the center of a vast plaza.

As they approached, the Stone in Isabella's hand began to glow, its light illuminating the path ahead. The archway shimmered with energy, the air thick with anticipation.

"This is it," Isabella said, her breath coming in quick gasps. "This is where it all begins."

Pablo was right beside her, his eyes scanning the surroundings. "Stay alert. Something feels off about this place."

Isabella nodded, her senses heightened. The Stone was reacting to the archway, its pulse quickening. But as they approached, the ground beneath them rumbled, and a low growl echoed through the water.

Suddenly, the air shimmered with dark energy, and the water around them began to churn violently.

The city was waking up.:

Chapter 16: The Last Loop

•	Final confrontation: a spiraling battle across all past timelines at once.

•	Isabella synchronizes with the Esmeralda, becoming its true keeper.

•	Rutherford is trapped in a time loop of his worst memories.

Chapter 16: The Guardians of Atlantis

The rumble of the earth beneath them intensified, sending waves of tension through Isabella's body. The air crackled with dark energy as if the very city itself were alive, waking from a millennia-long slumber. The water around her rippled violently, pulling her and Pablo apart as she struggled to keep her bearings.

"What's happening?" Pablo shouted over the comms, his voice tinged with panic.

"I don't know!" Isabella gasped. She grasped the glowing Esmeralda de Tiempo, its light now flickering erratically as the energy around them seemed to distort. "We've triggered something. The city—it's reacting to us!"

From the depths, a low growl echoed—deep, primal, and resonating through the water like the roar of some ancient beast. The sound reverberated through the stones of Atlantis, carrying with it a foreboding sense of danger. Isabella's heart raced as she looked up at the looming stone archway, which now shimmered with an ominous light.

"We need to move!" she urged Pablo, pulling him toward the arch. But as they swam closer, a powerful force suddenly surged from the water, knocking them both back.

Isabella gritted her teeth, fighting against the current, her mind racing. "What is this?" she thought, panic rising in her chest. The Stone pulsed in her hand again, the glowing light intensifying, as if it were responding to the threat in the city.

Just as she reached out to help Pablo regain his balance, the water ahead parted, and massive figures rose from the depths—figures draped in ceremonial armor, their faces obscured by ancient masks. They were tall, ethereal beings, their bodies shimmering with a faint, ghostly glow. Their movements were fluid, like the tides, and their eyes glowed with an eerie, unsettling blue.

"Guardians of the city," Camazotz's voice crackled through her earpiece, calm but urgent. "They were created to protect Atlantis and its secrets. They are ancient, and they will not let you pass."

Isabella's pulse quickened as the guardians moved toward them, their spears raised and pointed directly at her. The feeling of being hunted washed over her in waves.

"We don't have time for this!" she said through gritted teeth. "We have to get to the heart of the city and unlock the Stone's power. There's no other way!"

Pablo's deep voice echoed in her earpiece. "I can handle them. You just focus on the Stone. I'll make sure they don't get too close."

"Be careful," Isabella warned, watching as the guardians' ghostly figures slowly encircled them. She could feel the weight of their presence, an unspoken promise that they would not let her and her team advance without a fight.

Without another word, she let go of Pablo's arm and swam toward the heart of the city, her eyes locked on the glowing archway. The guardians closed in behind her, but she knew she couldn't stop. The Stone was pulsing with greater intensity, its energy beckoning her forward.

Pablo moved quickly behind her, his strong strokes propelling him through the water. "Go! I've got this!" he called out.

Isabella nodded, turning back to see Pablo charging toward the guardians. He was a blur of motion, his fists striking with precision, knocking the guardians back as he waded through their ethereal forms. They were strong, but he was relentless—his raw power a match for their ancient strength.

With every strike, the guardians' forms seemed to flicker, as though they were not entirely of this world. Isabella felt a pang of guilt, but there was no time to hesitate. The Stone was leading her to the heart of the city, and she couldn't afford to waste a moment.

She reached the archway, the energy around her growing colder as she passed beneath its towering stone frame. The air seemed to shift, and Isabella could feel the weight of time pressing in around her. This place, this ancient city, was more than just a lost civilization—it was a nexus, a point in time where the Stone's power could reshape history itself.

The moment she stepped into the inner sanctum, the guardians halted, their gaze fixed on her. She could feel their eyes, even though their faces were hidden behind the cold, expressionless masks. They were watching her, waiting, as if they could sense the power she wielded.

Ahead, at the far end of the chamber, was an enormous pedestal, bathed in light. On top of it lay a massive stone—its surface etched with intricate symbols that matched the ones on the Esmeralda de Tiempo. It was a second Stone, one that pulsed with energy, as though it were alive.

"Isabella," Camazotz's voice filled her earpiece once more. "That is the Heart Stone. It is the key to unlocking the full power of the Esmeralda. But be careful—touching it will trigger a series of trials. It will test you."

Isabella's heart raced. She knew the trials would not be easy. The Heart Stone had been guarded for centuries by those who believed its power was too great to be wielded by any mortal.

But Isabella was no longer just a mortal. The Esmeralda de Tiempo had chosen her, and she had come too far to turn back now.

With a steadying breath, she approached the pedestal. The guardians did not move; they merely watched her, silent and still, as if they understood the significance of this moment.

Isabella reached out, her fingers brushing the surface of the Heart Stone.

The moment her skin made contact with the stone, the world around her exploded into a kaleidoscope of light and sound. She felt herself pulled into the heart of the city, the very fabric of time and space unraveling before her. The trials had begun.

Chapter 17: A New Dawn in Chronic Bay

- Isabella returns—documented, empowered, now a professor of history.

- Pablo and Liberty continue working with her as protectors of the timeline.

- Camazotz disappears into myth once more.

Chapter 17: Trials of the Heart Stone

Isabella's fingers were still pressed against the Heart Stone when the world around her dissolved into a brilliant, blinding light. For a moment, she couldn't see, hear, or feel anything—only pure, overwhelming brilliance. Her heart raced, and she instinctively pulled her hand away from the stone, but it was too late. The light consumed her, and she was pulled into the unknown.

The darkness that followed was profound, and when her vision cleared, she found herself standing in an empty expanse, the ground beneath her cracked and desolate. The air was thick with tension, heavy with the weight of ancient power. A soft wind whispered through the ruins, carrying the scent of something forgotten, something old.

"Welcome, Isabella Monteverdi," a voice echoed, soft but commanding. "The Heart Stone has chosen you, but it will not give you its power freely. To wield it, you must face the trials. The first trial begins now."

The words were not spoken aloud; they vibrated in her mind, deep and resonant. She turned, looking around for the source, but saw nothing. Only the broken remnants of a city stretching out into infinity, its skyline like jagged teeth, frozen in time.

Suddenly, the ground shifted beneath her feet. A crack appeared, snaking across the barren landscape, and from it emerged a towering figure, draped in dark robes that shimmered like the night sky. The figure's face was hidden beneath a hood, but its presence was overwhelming, as though it were not merely a being but a force of nature itself.

"I am the Guardian of the First Trial," the figure intoned. "You will face your past, your regrets, and your fears. Only by confronting them can you hope to move forward."

Isabella's heart skipped a beat. The first trial was not a challenge of strength or intellect. It was a challenge of her soul.

Before she could respond, the air around her grew thick, and the world shifted again. The desolate landscape melted away, replaced by a memory—a vivid scene from her past.

She was back in Chronic Bay, standing outside the small, cramped apartment she shared with her mother. The sun was setting, casting a golden glow over the alley. She could hear the distant hum of traffic, the faint buzz of life in the city. Everything felt familiar—safe. But as her eyes moved to the door of the apartment, something shifted.

The door opened, and her mother stepped out, her face tired, but still smiling. Isabella could see the exhaustion in her eyes, the weight of the world that had never fully lifted from her shoulders. But before Isabella could call out to her, her mother's smile faded, and the door slammed shut.

Isabella's throat tightened. She had always wondered if she could have done more, if she could have made a difference for her mother. The guilt surged within her, sharp and suffocating. "I should have been there for you," she whispered to the empty air.

The figure of the Guardian appeared beside her, its voice low and cold. "This is your regret. You abandoned her when she needed you the most. You could have fought for her, fought for both of you. But instead, you ran. You chose to escape."

Isabella's eyes burned with unshed tears. "I didn't know how," she said, her voice cracking. "I didn't know what else to do. I thought I was protecting her, protecting myself. I thought..."

The Guardian's voice interrupted her. "And yet you chose to run. To leave her behind. To abandon everything you loved."

The weight of the words crushed her chest. The world around her shifted again, and she found herself standing on the edge of a cliff, looking out over a vast ocean. The wind howled around her, and the sun dipped beneath the horizon, casting long shadows across the water.

"Now," the Guardian said, "You must choose. Will you continue to flee from your past? Or will you face it head-on, accept the consequences of your actions, and move forward?"

Isabella's mind spun. She felt the weight of her past pushing down on her—her choices, her mistakes, the things she had left behind. But something stirred within her, a quiet strength that had been growing ever since she had taken the first step on this journey. She had already started facing her past, hadn't she? She had come to terms with her mistakes, and now, she was ready to make things right.

"I choose to face it," Isabella said, her voice steady and firm. "I'm done running."

The Guardian nodded, a faint flicker of approval crossing its hidden face. The world around Isabella began to dissolve, the ocean and the cliff fading away as the ground beneath her feet solidified once more.

"Well done," the Guardian said, its voice now softer, almost approving. "You have passed the first trial. But remember, this was only the beginning. The second trial will test your strength—not just physical strength, but the strength of your resolve, your will to change, to reshape your future."

Isabella nodded, her heart still pounding from the intensity of the first trial. "I'm ready for whatever comes next," she said, determination flooding through her veins.

The Guardian raised a hand, and the world around them shifted once again, the horizon bending and warping. The second trial awaited.

Chapter 18: The Echoes of Time

- A new codex is found by a child in the future.

 The legacy of the Esmeralda de Tiempo begins anew

Chapter 18: The Second Trial

The world before Isabella twisted and contorted, the landscape morphing into a new and unfamiliar scene. Gone was the desolate, ruined city of the first trial. Now, she stood in a place that felt entirely alien to her—yet, somehow, familiar. The air was thick with an unnatural chill, and dark clouds loomed overhead, casting an eerie shadow over the land. The ground was cracked and dry, stretching for miles in all directions. In the distance, she could make out a figure moving toward her, but it was obscured by the oppressive fog that seemed to rise from the ground.

The Guardian's voice cut through the silence, soft and reverberating. "This is the trial of strength. Not the strength of your body, but of your will. Your heart will be tested, Isabella Monteverdi. Will you fight for what you believe in, even when faced with impossible odds? Will you endure the pain of what you must sacrifice?"

The fog lifted slightly, revealing a vast expanse of twisted trees and jagged rocks. At the center of this eerie landscape stood a figure—a shadowy, imposing form. As it came into focus, Isabella's breath caught in her throat. It was herself. But not the woman she had become, strong and determined. This was a version of her she had feared—the one who had stayed silent, who had never fought back, the one who had once given up on everything. She was clad in tattered clothes, her face hollow with despair, her eyes empty.

"You," the figure rasped. "You left me behind. You abandoned everything that mattered."

Isabella felt her chest tighten. She knew this version of herself. It was the part of her that had fled Chronic Bay, the girl who had thought she couldn't handle the weight of her world. She had abandoned her community, her mother, and even herself. She had felt like a failure.

"That's not who I am anymore," Isabella said, her voice wavering but determined. "I've changed."

The shadowy version of herself stepped forward, its form flickering like a mirage. "Changed? You think you can just walk away from your past? The weakness you carry inside you, the doubts, they will always haunt you. You cannot outrun them."

Isabella clenched her fists. "I don't need to outrun them. I need to face them."

The figure laughed, the sound hollow and mocking. "Then prove it."

Without warning, the shadow lunged at her, its hands outstretched, aiming for her throat. Isabella instinctively stepped back, but the figure's speed was unnerving. It moved like a specter, a reflection of the doubts that had once consumed her.

Isabella didn't hesitate. She reached out and grabbed the shadow's wrist, forcing it back. But it wasn't just a physical fight. The shadow pressed against her mind, whispering her insecurities—her failures, her betrayals, the lies she had told herself. She stumbled, feeling the weight of her own self-doubt threatening to break her.

"You're nothing," the shadow hissed. "You've always been nothing."

Isabella shook her head, her chest tight with the force of the words. But something inside her shifted. The darkness of the trial, the reflection of her former self, was not the reality. It was just a mirror—a distortion of the past she could no longer allow to control her.

"I am something," she said through gritted teeth. "I am more than my mistakes. I am more than the person I was. I choose to be better."

With a surge of will, Isabella shoved the shadow back, feeling its grip on her mind loosen. She pushed against the suffocating weight of the past, refusing to let it claim her again. The shadow let out a cry of rage as it disintegrated into the fog, leaving Isabella standing alone on the cracked ground.

For a moment, there was silence. Then, the Guardian's voice returned, softer, more approving. "You have passed the second trial. You have shown strength—strength of character, strength of spirit. But remember, this is only the beginning. The path ahead will test you further. You must continue to fight—not just for yourself, but for everything you hold dear."

Isabella stood in the silence, her body trembling with the aftershocks of the trial. She felt drained, but a sense of clarity settled over her. She had faced her past. She had faced herself. And she had emerged stronger.

The world around her began to fade, the fog lifting as the trial came to an end. Isabella felt herself being pulled forward, back toward the reality she had left behind. She wasn't done yet. There was still much to be done, and she was more determined than ever to see her journey through.

Chapter 19: The Final Trial

The air shifted around Isabella as she felt herself pulled through the swirling currents of time once more. The world she had known, the desolate trial landscape, faded away, and in its place emerged something entirely different. This was no longer a barren wasteland or a twisted reflection of herself. No, this was something much more dangerous.

She stood at the edge of a vast, stormy ocean. The wind howled through her hair, tugging at her clothes, while the waves crashed violently against jagged rocks below. The sky was a chaotic blend of dark clouds and blinding flashes of lightning, illuminating the horizon in erratic bursts. In the distance, barely visible through the storm, was a towering, ancient stone structure. Its walls were covered in centuries-old runes, pulsing with an eerie glow.

The Guardian's voice resonated in the storm, its tone grave and final. "This is the third trial, Isabella Monteverdi—the trial of sacrifice. To pass, you must give up what you hold most dear. Only then will you possess the strength to wield the Esmeralda de Tiempo."

The words echoed in Isabella's mind. The trial of sacrifice. Her heart clenched. She had already faced her own past, stood strong against the darkest parts of herself. But now, she was being asked to give up something far more personal. Something that she wasn't sure she was ready to lose.

As she stood at the cliff's edge, a voice called to her from behind. "Isabella…"

She turned, her breath catching in her throat. It was Camazotz, the immortal wizard. He was standing behind her, his eyes filled with both wisdom and sorrow.

"You're ready, Isabella," he said softly. "But be prepared. This trial will test you in ways you cannot imagine."

The storm around them seemed to intensify at his words, the winds howling louder, the lightning flashing more violently. But Isabella could not tear her eyes away from Camazotz. Something about his presence made her feel grounded, as though she wasn't entirely alone in this trial. She reached out, but the moment her fingers brushed against his arm, he stepped back, fading into the mist.

"Camazotz!" she cried, her voice breaking. But it was too late. He was gone, lost to the storm.

The realization hit her then—whatever was coming next, she would have to face it alone.

The ground beneath her trembled, and the waters below began to churn. From the depths of the ocean, a dark figure began to emerge. It was an immense, shadowy beast, its form almost indistinguishable from the storm itself. Its glowing eyes locked onto Isabella with an intense hunger, and its massive jaws opened wide, revealing rows of razor-sharp teeth.

The Guardian spoke again, this time with a hint of urgency in its voice. "This creature is born from your fear of loss, Isabella. It is a manifestation of everything you are unwilling to sacrifice. You must defeat it to move forward. But remember, to do so, you must release what you hold most precious."

Isabella's heart raced. The beast roared, a sound that echoed like a thousand wails of torment. It was closing in, the very air thick with its presence. But she couldn't move. She couldn't fight. The Guardian's words gnawed at her—*what do I hold most dear?*

Her thoughts spiraled in every direction. She had so much to lose. Her life. Her family. The love she had for those she held close. The Esmeralda de Tiempo itself, the source of all this power, and the very reason she had come this far. But there was something deeper than that. The trials had stripped her bare. The past was gone, and the future felt uncertain, but she was not alone in her journey. She still had allies. They were her strength.

"Camazotz... Liberty... Pablo..." The names slipped from her lips, and in that moment, a powerful realization hit her. Her friends, her chosen family—they were everything. Her past, her struggles, they had all led her to this point. But to gain the power to protect them, to wield the Esmeralda de Tiempo to its fullest, she would have to make the ultimate choice.

The creature charged, its monstrous form moving with terrifying speed. Isabella could feel its power, its fury. But in that instant, something clicked. Her love for those she cared for, the people she had fought for, had become the very essence of her being. And as the beast lunged toward her, she understood what she needed to do.

With a cry of determination, she threw herself forward, toward the creature. At the last moment, just as it bore down on her, she pressed her hands to her chest, to her heart, and felt the Esmeralda de Tiempo pulse within her. She released her grip on everything—on her fear, her doubt, even her most precious memories—and let go.

The storm quieted.

The beast halted mid-attack, its glowing eyes flickering in confusion. The energy around Isabella flared, the power of the Esmeralda de

Tiempo washing over her like a wave. She felt an overwhelming peace, as though a great weight had been lifted from her shoulders.

And then, the creature vanished. Not destroyed, not defeated in the traditional sense—but transformed. It had been tamed, the fear turned to dust. The trial was over.

The Guardian's voice returned, now filled with an unmistakable sense of approval. "You have passed the third trial, Isabella Monteverdi. You have given up what you held most dear. Your sacrifice will guide you in the journey ahead."

Isabella stood in the calm that followed the storm, her heart racing but her mind clear. The Esmeralda de Tiempo now rested firmly within her, no longer a distant relic but a powerful part of her very soul. She had faced her trials. She had emerged victorious.

But the journey was far from over. With the Esmeralda de Tiempo at her side, she had only begun to understand its power. And there were still those who would stop at nothing to claim it for themselves.

The storm had subsided, but the true battle was yet to come.

Chapter 20: The Edge of Time

Isabella stood at the precipice, the Esmeralda de Tiempo pulsing in her palm, its light flickering in tune with her heartbeat. The storm had passed, but the weight of the trials lingered. Her body ached, her mind stretched thin from the intense battles she had faced—both internal and external. The calm after the storm felt unsettling, as though the universe itself was holding its breath, waiting for what would come next.

The ancient stone tower loomed ahead, its doors now wide open, beckoning her into the unknown. Isabella could feel the presence of something—someone—waiting for her inside. She had come so far, but each step felt heavier than the last, as though the very fabric of time itself was pulling her toward a final confrontation.

Before she could take another step, a voice called out from behind her. "Isabella."

She spun, her heart racing. Standing in the distance, framed by the broken clouds, was Camazotz. His form shimmered, like a specter pulled from the ether. He hadn't been with her in the final trial, but here he was, returned at the moment she needed him most.

"You're here," Isabella said, her voice cracking with emotion. "I thought… I thought I was alone."

"You were never alone," Camazotz replied, his voice like a soothing wind, calm yet carrying the weight of centuries. "You have always had the strength within you. The Esmeralda de Tiempo has chosen you. You have faced your fears, your past. But now, you must face what lies ahead. You cannot do it alone."

Isabella swallowed hard, the implications of his words settling over her like a heavy fog. "What lies ahead?" she asked, her voice barely a whisper.

"The final choice," Camazotz said gravely. "The Esmeralda de Tiempo holds unimaginable power, but that power comes with a cost. To wield it fully, you must decide what you are willing to sacrifice—and what you are willing to protect. The forces that seek it will not stop, Isabella. And there are still trials you must face, but these will be unlike any before. This time, the stakes are higher."

Isabella nodded slowly, understanding dawning on her. The battle wasn't over. The final confrontation loomed on the horizon, and it would be the most dangerous yet.

"You are ready," Camazotz said, as though reading her thoughts. "But you must not forget what you have learned. Time is a fragile thing. It can be manipulated, bent, or broken. But there are consequences. The choices you make now will echo through all of time, and there is no going back."

With that, Camazotz began to fade, his form dissolving into the mist. "The path you choose is yours, Isabella. But remember—nothing in time is ever truly lost. And nothing in time is ever fully yours."

Isabella stood alone once more, staring at the open doors of the stone tower. The weight of her destiny pressed down on her chest, but she was no longer afraid. She had faced the trials. She had let go of her fears. Now, she had to embrace what lay ahead—no matter the cost.

Taking a deep breath, she stepped forward, her heart steady, her grip on the Esmeralda de Tiempo firm. The tower seemed to breathe with life, its ancient walls pulsing with energy as if it, too, was aware of the momentous choice before her.

Inside, the air was thick with the scent of incense and old stone. The flickering light of countless candles illuminated the path ahead, casting long shadows that seemed to stretch toward her like hungry hands. In the center of the room stood a pedestal, upon which rested a book bound in weathered leather. It was open, its pages covered in intricate symbols that Isabella could not yet decipher.

As she approached, the book's pages began to turn on their own, the symbols shifting and rearranging before her eyes. It was as if the very fabric of reality was bending to the will of the Esmeralda de Tiempo.

A voice, ancient and cold, echoed through the chamber. "You have come, Isabella Monteverdi. You are the one the Esmeralda has chosen. But be warned—the choices you make here will shape the future. Will you protect the flow of time, or will you seize its power for yourself?"

Isabella's heart raced. The voice was familiar yet unrecognizable, a blend of countless whispers from ages long past. The guardian of the tower, perhaps. She had no idea what lay within the pages of that book, but she knew one thing for certain: this was the moment where everything would change.

The chamber seemed to vibrate with the weight of the decision. Behind her, the doors slammed shut, trapping her within the ancient stone walls. The only path forward was to confront whatever lay in the pages of the book, whatever the Esmeralda de Tiempo had prepared for her.

Isabella's breath quickened as she reached for the book, her fingers brushing against its pages. The symbols shifted again, this time forming an image: a vision of the future. A future that could be shaped by her actions.

The voice spoke again, louder this time, as though trying to reach the depths of her soul. "The future is a fragile thing. To change it, to control it, requires sacrifice. What will you give, Isabella Monteverdi? What will you protect?"

The words echoed in her mind, and for the first time, she realized the true weight of her choices. This wasn't just about saving the present, or the people she loved. It was about shaping the very fabric of time itself.

Her eyes locked onto the image in the book—a vision of the future, of a world torn apart by chaos, ruled by those who sought to control the Esmeralda de Tiempo for their own ends. A world where time itself had been fractured, its balance destroyed.

In that moment, Isabella understood. She could protect the timeline, protect the world, but to do so would require giving up everything. The power of the Esmeralda de Tiempo was immense, but it was also a double-edged sword. In wielding it, she would be bound to it forever.

A single tear slid down her cheek as she reached for the book again, the weight of the decision settling over her like a cold, unshakable burden.

The final trial had begun.

Chapter 21: The Price of Time

Isabella stood before the book, the air around her thick with anticipation, every inch of her body on alert. The Esmeralda de Tiempo in her hand pulsed, a steady rhythm, almost like a heartbeat that echoed in the silence of the chamber. Its power hummed beneath her skin, urging her forward. But now, more than ever, she understood the gravity of the choice she was about to make.

The vision from the book haunted her—the world in ruins, torn apart by those who would twist time to their own will. The power to reshape the past, to control the future, to rewrite everything she knew. The temptation was overwhelming. But with it, she knew came a cost—one she could not yet comprehend.

A distant, cold laugh echoed through the chamber, shaking her from her thoughts. It was followed by a voice, smooth and calculated.

"So, you've made it this far," Judge Rutherford's voice reverberated, carrying the same chilling authority she had heard before, in her darkest moments. "But you can't hide forever, Isabella. Time will find you. It always does."

She spun around, eyes narrowing as she searched the shadows. Her heart hammered against her ribs. How had he found her? And what did he want now?

From the depths of the shadows emerged the imposing figure of Judge Malcolm Rutherford, his presence radiating an unsettling calm. His usual sharp, authoritative expression was now a mask of pure malice. In his hands, he held a dark, swirling orb—a manifestation of the corrupted energy he had drawn from manipulating time itself.

"You think you can stop me?" Rutherford continued, his voice thick with disdain. "I've spent my entire life learning to bend time to my will. The Esmeralda de Tiempo was meant for someone like me, someone who understands its true power. But you... you've meddled with forces you can't even begin to grasp."

Isabella's grip on the stone tightened. "You don't understand what you're dealing with," she said, her voice steady despite the pounding in her chest. "This power isn't for someone like you. It was never meant to be used for control or manipulation."

Rutherford chuckled, a bitter, humorless sound that echoed through the chamber. "You misunderstand, Isabella. I know exactly what I'm doing. Time is nothing more than a tool to shape the world as it should be. You, like everyone else, are too naïve to see that. I intend to fix this broken world, and with the Esmeralda de Tiempo in my grasp, I will bend it to my will."

The orb in his hand glowed brighter, sending waves of distorted energy into the air. Isabella could feel the heat of it, the raw force that threatened to overwhelm her. His power was no longer just a shadow—it was tangible, pressing against her like a weight she could barely bear.

"I won't let you destroy everything," Isabella said, her voice hardening as she stepped toward him. "I've already seen what happens when time is used recklessly. I won't let you tear apart the future to satisfy your need for control."

Rutherford's expression twisted with contempt. "You still don't understand, do you? Time is power. And power must be wielded by those who know how to control it. Not by someone who—" He paused, his eyes narrowing as he noticed the subtle glow emanating from the Esmeralda de Tiempo in her hand.

"You're already too late, Rutherford," she said, her voice rising with conviction. The Esmeralda de Tiempo began to pulse, its light intensifying, answering her will.

Rutherford's eyes flickered with a mix of fury and realization. "No…" he breathed. "You don't know what you're doing. You're playing with forces beyond your understanding."

With a sudden motion, Rutherford raised the orb in his hand, and a blast of dark energy shot toward Isabella, but she was ready. The Esmeralda de Tiempo flared to life, its light colliding with the darkness in a brilliant burst of energy.

The impact shook the very foundations of the tower, sending a shockwave through the air. Isabella staggered but held her ground, her hand gripping the Esmeralda de Tiempo as if her life depended on it. And perhaps it did.

The room was filled with the crackling of energy, the two forces locked in a battle of wills. Isabella felt the full weight of the Esmeralda's power coursing through her, felt the future, the past, and every moment in between, all colliding in her mind. She saw timelines unravel, futures splintering, destinies shifting like sand in the wind.

But in that chaos, she found clarity.

"You want to control time, Rutherford?" Isabella called out, her voice rising above the storm of energy swirling around them. "You want to reshape it to fit your vision? Then know this—you can't control what you don't understand."

With that, she focused all of her will into the Esmeralda de Tiempo, channeling its energy through her body, pulling from every lesson, every sacrifice, every moment of growth she had endured on this journey. The stone flared brighter than ever before, blinding in its intensity.

The blast of light that followed was pure, unyielding. It cut through the darkness like a blade, striking Rutherford with a force that sent him crashing backward, his orb shattering into pieces. The chamber shook violently, but Isabella stood firm, the light from the Esmeralda de Tiempo enveloping her like a protective shield.

Rutherford's body lay motionless on the ground, his form crumpled and defeated. The air grew still.

Isabella breathed heavily, her hands trembling as the light from the stone began to dim, its power settling. The Esmeralda de Tiempo was no longer a weapon, but a symbol of what she had become—of the choices she had made, and the person she had chosen to be.

But even in the silence, she knew this was not the end. There would be more to come, more challenges to face. The future was never set in stone.

Isabella turned away from Rutherford's defeated form, her gaze falling on the book that still lay open before her. The pages, now blank, began to fill once more, the symbols shifting as though waiting for her to make the final decision.

"Isabella," came Camazotz's voice, calm and steady in her mind. "You've faced the darkness. Now, choose the light."

She took a deep breath, her eyes locked on the words before her, and made her choice.

The future was in her hands.

Chapter 22: The Reckoning of Time

Isabella's breath was shallow, her heart a drumbeat that echoed through the stillness of the chamber. The Esmeralda de Tiempo was warm in her hand, its light dimming, as though it too were catching its breath. The pages of the book that had once seemed so inscrutable were now alive, twisting and shifting, awaiting the next stroke of destiny.

She stared at the blank space on the page where the future had been, contemplating what came next. In the moments of clarity that had come from her battle with Rutherford, she had seen not just what was possible, but what was inevitable. The past had been reshaped; the present was malleable. But what about the future? Could she choose it? Or was she, too, bound by the same rules as everyone else?

"Isabella," Camazotz's voice broke through her thoughts, gentle yet urgent. "Time is a river, not a still pool. The flow of it cannot be controlled by a single hand, no matter how strong or skilled. You may shape moments, but the river will always find its way. You must decide: will you shape the future for all, or will you leave it untouched?"

She felt the weight of his words, the depth of their meaning settling in her chest like a stone. The future—the world beyond this moment—had always seemed so distant, so abstract. But now it felt closer, more immediate. And in that moment, she knew: her choice wasn't just about time. It was about freedom.

The book seemed to pulse as though waiting for her to decide. Each turn of the page before her was a choice that would shape the world in ways she could never predict. The weight of it was almost too much to bear. The power to control time. The power to create a future, or to destroy it.

"You know what you must do," came the voice again. This time it was not Camazotz, but Liberty. Her voice was sharp, clear, and full of the kind of wisdom that only a young prodigy could possess.

Isabella turned toward her, her eyes searching for the familiar face. Liberty stood just outside the circle of light, her gaze unwavering, her arms folded as she watched Isabella carefully. Despite everything they had been through, despite the chaos, Liberty's confidence in Isabella remained. The teen had always seen something in her, something Isabella hadn't fully understood until now.

Liberty spoke again, her voice softer this time. "You can't hold the future in your hands. The world will change, no matter what you choose. You've seen it—how time bends and shifts, how everything is connected. But that doesn't mean you have to control it. Sometimes, the best thing to do is to let it flow."

Isabella nodded slowly, her fingers tightening around the stone. It felt heavier now. Not because of the power it held, but because of the responsibility it demanded.

Pablo's voice rang out from behind her, startling her. "We're with you, Isabella. You don't have to do this alone."

She turned to him, meeting his gaze. His face was set with determination, his posture strong and solid. After everything they had been through—after their battles, their losses—Pablo had become more than just an ally. He was family. And that was all the strength she needed to make her choice.

The Esmeralda de Tiempo pulsed again, this time with a deep resonance that filled the room. She could feel its power coursing through her, like an electric current that threatened to overwhelm her senses. Time itself seemed to hang in the balance, waiting on her decision.

Isabella closed her eyes and took a deep breath, the world around her going quiet as she allowed herself to sink into the moment. She saw the ripple effect of every action she had taken, every choice she had made. And in that silence, she understood.

Time was not meant to be controlled by one person. It was a living, breathing force that belonged to all. And no matter how much power she had in her hands, no matter how much control she could grasp, the truth was clear: she couldn't hold it back. Not forever. The future needed to be free.

She opened her eyes, looking once more at the blank pages of the book. The words began to form, slowly at first, then with increasing speed. The future was writing itself. Not by her hand, but by the choices of everyone who would come after.

Her hand trembled as she let the Esmeralda de Tiempo fall to the floor, the stone's glow fading as it settled in the dust. It had served its purpose. It had shown her the power of choice, and now it was time to let go.

"Time will flow as it should," she whispered to herself. "And I will live in it. With it."

The air seemed to shift, as if the very fabric of reality had bent with her decision. A warm, steady wind swept through the chamber, as though the universe itself was exhaling a breath it had been holding for too long.

"Isabella," Camazotz's voice was softer now, tinged with something almost like pride. "You've done what few others could. You have let time flow freely. And in doing so, you have embraced your place in it."

She turned toward him, meeting his ancient eyes with a newfound sense of understanding. The immortal wizard, who had once been so distant, now seemed like a figure of wisdom—a guide who had helped her find her path.

The others stood with her, their faces a mix of exhaustion and resolve. They had all played their part in this journey. And now, it was time for them to move forward, together, into the unknown.

"We've made it this far," Liberty said, breaking the silence. "Now, we get to write the rest of our stories."

Isabella smiled, a true smile, one that reached all the way to her soul. The weight that had been pressing down on her for so long had finally lifted. She was no longer bound by the fear of what might happen next. She was free.

And with that, they stepped into the future—into the next chapter of their lives.

Chapter 23: The Unwritten Path

The world around them shimmered with the quiet hum of possibility, as if reality itself had taken a deep breath and now exhaled, waiting for the next movement. The chamber that had been the setting of their most pivotal moments was now behind them. The Esmeralda de Tiempo, once a heavy weight in Isabella's hands, had slipped from their grasp. Its power, while immense, had never been the true measure of control.

The true measure, Isabella realized, was the way they moved forward.

"Where do we go now?" Liberty asked, her voice betraying none of the uncertainty that seemed to swirl around them all. She was always the one to ask the question, to push for the next step. Her curiosity, unshaken by the dangers they had faced, was a constant source of inspiration.

Pablo cracked his knuckles, the weight of the journey finally catching up to him. The muscles that had once been taut with tension now hung more relaxed, the constant alertness they had all lived with gradually easing. "I've been thinking. If this is the moment we get to choose the future... What's the point of fighting if we don't make sure everyone has the chance to fight for themselves?"

"He's right," Camazotz said, his ancient eyes narrowing as if the weight of time itself had finally begun to settle in him as well. "The future was never meant to be shaped by the few. You have made your choices, and the paths that will come from them will ripple out into history. But you must now decide what part you play in that future."

Isabella stared out into the distance, her thoughts swirling. The future was no longer just an abstract concept; it was a space she could shape—more importantly, it was a space they all could shape. She had seen too many moments in time where people had been forced into corners, their paths dictated by those who held power over them. Judge Rutherford's obsession with control had nearly shattered everything. She wouldn't let the same thing happen again.

"We help them," Isabella said, her voice steady but full of purpose. "The people who've never had a choice. The ones whose stories weren't written. We help them write their own futures."

Liberty nodded, her bright eyes sparking with a shared determination. "But we can't do it alone. The knowledge we've gained, the skills we have—together, we can build something. But we need others, people who can push the world toward that change."

"Agreed," Pablo chimed in. "We've seen the worst of what happens when the wrong people are in charge. It's time to stand up for the ones who've been trampled underfoot."

Isabella could see the world ahead, not in terms of the grand battles or the grand gestures, but in the small acts—the choices made every day by people with the courage to change their lives. What had once seemed impossible now felt so very close. It was there, in the choices they made, that the true power of time revealed itself.

"The Stone," Camazotz said, his voice low and contemplative. "Though it is no longer in your hands, its legacy remains. You are its true bearers now, Isabella. You, and those who stand with you."

She turned to him, feeling a sense of finality but also something else—something deeper, an undercurrent of potential. "We all are," she said softly. "The power isn't in the stone. It never was. It's in the people who choose to stand up, no matter the odds."

They walked away from the chamber, leaving the past behind as they stepped into the future. The air around them seemed lighter now, as if the world itself had been waiting for them to step forward, waiting for them to decide what they were truly capable of.

The streets of the city felt different. The hum of the bustling world was no longer just noise but a collective heartbeat. People moved past them, their faces a mixture of hope and uncertainty. They weren't looking for a hero. They weren't even looking for someone to lead them. They were simply trying to live their lives, to build a future of their own making. And that was something Isabella could understand now.

Liberty, as always, was the first to break the silence. "So... now what?"

Isabella smiled, her heart lighter than it had been in a long time. "Now, we build. Together."

It wasn't just about stopping Judge Rutherford anymore. It wasn't just about finding a way to wield power—it was about creating a world where that power didn't need to be wielded at all. A world where people didn't need to fear the future because they could shape it for themselves. That was the gift she had gained from the Esmeralda de Tiempo.

And it was the gift she intended to give back to the world.

Chapter 24: Building the Future

The sun dipped low, casting long shadows across the streets of Chronic Bay. Isabella stood by the window of their makeshift headquarters, watching the people below. There was an energy to the city now, a pulse that hadn't been there before. It was subtle, but it was there. People moved with purpose, as if they had been given permission to dream again.

Behind her, Liberty was pacing, fingers tapping on her phone screen, running through calculations and diagrams. "The tech's almost ready. We can start distributing the knowledge we've gained—teach people how to access the systems, how to bypass the old barriers that held them back."

Pablo, sitting in a worn armchair by the wall, rubbed his chin thoughtfully. "We've all seen what happens when too much power's concentrated in the wrong hands. But if we spread the tools to the people, give them the knowledge to create their own futures... it changes everything."

"It does," Camazotz said, his deep voice reverberating through the room like the echoes of ancient wisdom. He stood with his back to them, gazing out the same window Isabella had been at moments before, as if searching for something in the distance. "But remember, change comes with its own challenges. The powers that were in control—the ones who wanted the Esmeralda de Tiempo for themselves—they're not just going to disappear. Power never gives up easily."

Isabella turned to face him, the weight of his words settling in her mind. She had been so focused on what came next, on how to rebuild and create something better. She hadn't stopped to think about the forces that would still oppose them—the remnants of the old world, those who would rather control than liberate.

"We're ready for that fight," she said, her voice stronger now, steadier than it had been in the past. "We've been preparing for this."

"True," Pablo agreed. "But we can't afford to be cocky. It's not about fighting one battle; it's about fighting a war of persistence."

Liberty paused her pacing and looked up at Isabella. "We have one thing they don't. Unity. We're not just a group anymore; we're a movement. The more people we bring into the fold, the harder it will be for them to stamp us out."

Isabella's eyes softened as she nodded. It had been hard to see the strength of their alliance at first, as the chaos of the Stone and the forces of Rutherford had dominated their thoughts. But now, as they looked ahead, she realized that it wasn't just the people in this room who mattered. It was everyone who believed in the future they could create. It was the millions of others who had been oppressed, silenced, kept from reaching their potential.

"I've been thinking about that," she said, a plan forming in her mind. "We can't just work from the shadows anymore. We need to be out in the open. We need to give people something to rally around. Something more than just the promise of change—we need them to see what's possible when we all fight together."

Liberty set her phone down, eyes sparkling with excitement. "A public launch? Something that shows everyone how we can disrupt the old system, how we can bring access and equality back into the hands of the people?"

"Exactly," Isabella replied. "If we're going to rebuild, it's not just about the technology. It's about showing the people the strength they have within themselves to create change. We all have the power to shape our world."

"To ignite the spark," Camazotz murmured, more to himself than anyone else.

Isabella looked at her team, the people who had become her family over the course of their journey. "We've been given the chance to reshape the future. Let's not waste it. Let's give the people the tools, the knowledge, and the belief in themselves they need to take control."

She turned back to the window. The streets below felt alive in a way that was new to her. A movement had started. It was still small, still fragile—but it was real. The flickering light of possibility burned bright, and it would only grow stronger from here.

The future was not yet written. But it would be.

Chapter 25: The Spark Ignites

The weight of their plan hung heavy in the air as Isabella and her team gathered in their makeshift command center. Liberty had been busy setting up secure networks, digging into old systems, and patching together anything that would allow them to connect with the world in ways that had been inaccessible before. Pablo, ever the strategist, had been mapping out a path to take their message public without drawing too much unwanted attention. Camazotz had been quieter than usual, reflecting on the intricacies of the ancient forces still at play in the world around them.

Isabella paced the floor, her mind racing with the final pieces of the puzzle. "We're almost there. If we pull this off, the world will never look the same again."

Pablo stood from his seat by the table, stretching his broad shoulders. "We've got one shot at this, and we need to make it count. We can't afford to be sloppy."

Liberty cracked a grin, her fingers tapping away on her tablet. "Sloppy isn't in our vocabulary." She looked up, a glint of determination in her eyes. "I've been working on the tech. If we're going to make this go viral, we need to hit every social channel, every underground network—hit them where they least expect it."

"And," Camazotz added, "we must be sure that this message is more than just a tool. It must be a symbol. Symbols transcend time and space. They resonate in ways information cannot."

Isabella nodded, turning her gaze toward the large map of the city they'd spread out on the wall. Dots and lines marked places they'd need to hit, places where the resistance could make the greatest impact.

"Everything hinges on this," Isabella said, her voice quieter now. "We can't just give people a blueprint for change. We have to show them what that change can look like. We need to remind them of their power. Of their agency."

Pablo raised an eyebrow. "And how do we plan on doing that?"

Isabella smiled, a quiet fire kindling within her. "We'll give them a vision—something worth fighting for. Not just promises. We'll give them something they can hold on to, something that makes them feel like they're part of something bigger than themselves."

Liberty's fingers flew over her tablet as she pulled up a map of global social platforms and underground communication networks. "I'm starting to get the message boards synced. With the right push, we could see the kind of viral wave that shakes the system."

"Make sure we stay under the radar," Pablo warned, glancing over her shoulder. "The last thing we need is Judge Rutherford or his people catching wind of what we're doing. We can't have them tracing us back."

Isabella turned back to the map. "I've been thinking. The core of what we're fighting for is not just technology, not just access—it's freedom. Freedom to choose, freedom to live beyond the reach of those who want to control us. We need to make sure that everyone—every single person out there—understands that."

"Freedom," Camazotz said softly, his voice resonating with something ancient. "A force more powerful than time itself. But freedom is never free. It comes at a price. You must be prepared for what follows."

The room grew still, the weight of his words settling in their minds.

"Then we make sure the price is worth it," Isabella said firmly. "We have no choice. We either move forward, or we let them win."

The team worked late into the night, finalizing details, prepping their message. Liberty had crafted a digital manifesto—simple, bold, direct. It would go live on every channel, every platform, pushing the message of freedom and unity. A call to action. A spark that could ignite the flames of revolution.

As dawn broke, they stood in front of the screens, watching the first wave of their message take hold. The internet lit up, like a network of stars bursting into life. Social media, encrypted forums, digital newsfeeds—they all began to hum with activity. The hashtags began trending, the images began to circulate. Thousands—no, millions—were starting to share their message.

The first comment they saw—an anonymous user—was simple, and it was enough.

"We can do this. We will fight back."

Isabella felt a knot loosen in her chest. It was happening.

But with the rush of success came a sharp realization—their enemies wouldn't sit idly by.

"Rutherford is going to come after us with everything he's got," Pablo said, his voice grim. "We have to be ready."

Isabella nodded. "We will be. We have to keep moving, keep pushing. We've awakened the people, and now we lead them."

They had taken the first step. But the path ahead was still uncertain, fraught with danger. Rutherford's reach extended further than they could see, and they would have to stay one step ahead if they were going to succeed.

But for the first time in a long while, Isabella felt the weight of their mission settle into a comfortable space. They had started a movement—no longer confined to the shadows, no longer outnumbered by the forces of oppression. They were not alone in this fight.

The people were with them.

And that was enough.

Chapter 26: The Tide Turns

The days following the digital manifesto's release were a whirlwind. Isabella barely had time to process the success before the world seemed to flip upside down. The message had spread like wildfire, but with that fire came smoke—the kind that burned and choked. Rutherford had not wasted a second. His resources were vast, his reach global. It didn't take long for his agents to start hunting for the source of the uprising, scouring encrypted channels, pulling strings behind the scenes.

Liberty's eyes were glued to the screens in front of her, her fingers tapping quickly as she worked on new security measures. "They're closing in," she muttered. "I've seen their patterns. They're not just following the message—they're triangulating the signal."

Isabella stood behind her, her mind whirring with the information. "Can we mask it?"

Liberty hesitated for only a moment before shaking her head. "Not indefinitely. We're going to need more time, and they're moving fast. They've already started to shut down the underground forums."

"How long until we're exposed?" Isabella asked, her voice steady but taut with urgency.

"A few days, maybe less," Liberty said, her tone grim. "They're coming for us. And they're bringing everything they have."

Isabella turned toward the map on the wall. It was a giant matrix of cities, countries, and key resistance points they had rallied to their cause. She could almost feel the pulse of the world, flickering with hope, but also with a dangerous undercurrent of fear. Rutherford's control was not just political—it was psychological. The longer they operated in the shadows, the more dangerous their fight would become. It was only a matter of time before he found them.

"Then we don't hide. We move forward." Isabella's voice rang with an unshakable certainty. "We fight fire with fire."

Pablo, who had been pacing the room, stopped and turned to face her. "What are you thinking?"

"People are scared," Isabella said, glancing at each of them. "But they're not helpless. They have power. We just need to show them that." She walked over to the table where a holographic map of the world flickered. "We've got key resistance points—places where we can launch coordinated counterattacks. We'll force Rutherford to spread his resources thin. He can't control everything."

"That's risky," Camazotz interjected. His voice, always so calm, held a note of warning. "Rutherford's reach is vast, and if you push too hard, too fast, you risk exposing the people who rely on us."

"I know," Isabella said, nodding. "But we have to show them we're not afraid. We need to go on the offensive. If we wait, we're going to be sitting ducks."

Liberty shifted in her seat, an idea sparking in her eyes. "What if we escalate in waves? We hit key communication hubs, broadcast encrypted messages about their atrocities. Make it impossible for them to ignore it. The world will see Rutherford for who he really is."

Isabella's gaze locked on Liberty's. "And we do it with style. We make it impossible for anyone to look away."

"That's... actually brilliant," Pablo said, leaning forward. "We control the narrative before they can."

Camazotz considered it for a moment. "But remember, Isabella, every action has a consequence. When you engage with forces like Rutherford's, you're not just fighting against them—you're also fighting against the system they've built. It's not just about defeating them. It's about breaking the chains that keep the world in fear."

"Then let's break them," Isabella said, her resolve hardening. "We'll show them how powerful they really are. And we'll fight until every last chain is shattered."

The next few days were a blur of action. Isabella's plan began to take shape, a coordinated global effort to strike back at Rutherford's chokehold on communication. Liberty worked around the clock, creating encrypted broadcasts that would target major media channels while keeping their identities hidden. Pablo and Camazotz worked on logistics, gathering local resistance cells and training them for a variety of defensive measures.

As they began their first wave of coordinated attacks, the resistance spread word to local communities, empowering them to take action. In the streets of major cities—New York, London, Mexico City— underground broadcasts flashed across billboards and screens, interrupting the usual flow of propaganda with the stark truth of Rutherford's actions. It was raw, unfiltered, and to the point: a declaration that the world was no longer controlled by fear.

But the backlash came fast.

Within hours, Rutherford's forces retaliated with all the fury they could muster. They ramped up surveillance, cracked down on social media accounts, and sent agents to hunt down those who had helped spread the resistance's message. Agents combed the streets in search of those who had participated in the rebellion, and the air was thick with tension.

In a dingy apartment in New York, the team watched as the fallout began to unfold on their screens.

"Rutherford's people are closing in on the message hubs," Liberty said, her fingers moving frantically as she attempted to reroute some of the broadcast signals. "He's hitting back hard."

"Can we keep it up?" Isabella asked, her gaze never leaving the screen.

"For now, yeah," Liberty answered. "But we're running out of time before they locate us."

"We can't stop," Isabella said, standing and pacing once more. "We keep pushing. We make sure the people know what's happening. We remind them that they can't be silenced."

Pablo's phone buzzed in his pocket, and he pulled it out, scanning the message that had just arrived. His face went pale. "It's worse than we thought. Rutherford's agents are targeting the underground cells. They've hit several safe houses already."

Isabella's heart raced. The realization hit her hard—they were no longer just fighting for their lives. They were fighting for the lives of the very people who had helped them. Every minute they wasted now could cost someone their future.

"We move now," Isabella said, determination in her eyes. "We protect those who stood with us, and we keep fighting. Rutherford won't win this war. Not if we're all in this together."

Chapter 27: The Walls Closing In

The aftermath of the first wave of resistance broadcasts left the world in a chaotic swirl of fear and hope. Isabella stood at the window of their temporary safe house, watching as the lights of the city flickered like distant stars. The sense of urgency in the air was palpable, suffocating. The resistance had made its mark, but at what cost?

Her thoughts were interrupted by a sharp knock on the door. Liberty entered first, her expression tight, as if something heavy weighed on her shoulders. Behind her, Pablo and Camazotz followed, their faces just as grim.

"They've found the safe houses," Liberty said without preamble, her voice strained. "Rutherford's agents have raided four more locations in the past two hours."

Isabella felt her stomach drop. "And our allies?"

Liberty shook her head. "We lost contact with a few of them. I don't know if they've been captured or just went dark to avoid detection. But we're running out of places to hide. We're compromised."

"We can't back down now," Isabella said firmly. She turned away from the window, facing her team. "We've opened the floodgates.

We've shown the world the truth. We can't stop just because Rutherford is making a move. We have to go on the offensive."

Pablo stepped forward, a frown deepening on his face. "Isabella, the truth is, we're getting cornered. We don't have enough people to keep up with the raids, and we can't keep hiding in safe houses forever."

"I know," she said quietly, her heart heavy with the weight of their struggle. "But if we stop now, everything we've fought for will be lost. We need to find a way to turn the tables."

Camazotz's voice, as calm as always, cut through the tension. "You are right, Isabella. You have given the world hope, but hope without action is fragile. You need to hit Rutherford where it hurts."

"Where?" Liberty asked, her hands moving over her tablet as if trying to pull answers from the very air.

"He's vulnerable," Camazotz continued, his eyes narrowing with ancient wisdom. "Not just physically, but politically. The world sees him as a tyrant, but his position is built on secrecy. If you expose the corruption at the heart of his empire—his dealings with the elites, his manipulation of the system—you will break the chain."

Isabella nodded. The pieces were falling into place. "His control comes from fear and secrecy. If we shatter that, if we force him into the open, we can destabilize his power. We'll make him answer to the people."

Liberty's eyes widened as the plan unfolded in her mind. "You're talking about pulling back the curtain completely. We use the media we've already disrupted to expose the corruption at the highest levels."

"Exactly," Isabella said, feeling a rush of adrenaline course through her. "We don't just target his agents. We target the system that enables him. We show the world how deep his corruption goes."

Pablo clenched his fists, the anger in his eyes evident. "And once we expose it, we fight back. We hit him where it hurts most. We take away his grip on the people."

Isabella turned to Camazotz. "Can you help us get access to the information we need? Something that will shake the foundation of his rule?"

The ancient wizard nodded slowly, his expression thoughtful. "I can open the way, but be prepared. The deeper you go, the more dangerous it becomes. Rutherford has hidden his secrets well, and those who protect him will stop at nothing to keep them buried."

"We don't have a choice," Isabella said, her voice hardening. "It's all or nothing now."

The team worked quickly, fueled by the fire of their mission. Liberty cracked encrypted files, searching for the one leak that could unravel Rutherford's empire. Pablo and Camazotz made plans to infiltrate key institutions where Rutherford's financial and political influence was strongest. Isabella prepared to address the people once more, knowing that their next broadcast would be the most dangerous one yet.

As Liberty typed furiously, her eyes narrowed in concentration, she finally let out a breath of relief. "I've found it."

Isabella moved over to her, leaning over her shoulder to see the glowing screen. "What is it?"

"A list of offshore accounts, investments in corrupt governments, and illegal deals with some of the most powerful figures in the world," Liberty explained. "This is the kind of information that would destroy Rutherford if it gets out."

"And we can get it to the world?" Isabella asked, her heart pounding with the weight of their next move.

"We can," Liberty said, her voice unwavering. "But we have to act fast. If Rutherford discovers that we've found this, it's game over."

"Then we don't waste time," Isabella said, her resolve hardening. "We broadcast this to every network we can reach."

They worked through the night, preparing for the broadcast. It was their most dangerous move yet, but it was the only way forward. At dawn, they set their plan into motion.

The world watched as the familiar screens flickered to life. Isabella stood at the center of the broadcast, her face resolute and unflinching. The weight of the moment hung heavy in the air.

"People of the world," she began, her voice carrying through the broadcast, "you've been lied to. You've been told that your lives are dictated by a system beyond your control. But that system, the one that has kept you oppressed, is built on a foundation of corruption and secrecy."

Behind her, images flashed on the screen—offshore accounts, illegal trades, photos of Rutherford shaking hands with the world's most corrupt leaders.

"This is the truth," Isabella continued. "Rutherford's empire is nothing but a house of cards. And today, we've pulled it down."

The broadcast continued, showing the full extent of Rutherford's dealings, implicating not just him but the network of power that had kept him in control for so long. When it ended, the world was silent.

Then, the chaos began.

As expected, Rutherford's forces responded with fury. They launched a full-scale manhunt for the resistance, hunting down every lead, every whisper of their location. But the damage was done. The truth had been exposed, and there was no going back. The people were awake. They were no longer passive. They were rising.

But as the storm of retaliation grew, Isabella knew one thing for certain—the fight had just begun.

Chapter 28: The Price of Truth

The city was awake. People who had been silent for too long now moved in droves, shouting, chanting, and demanding justice. The streets of New York, once a labyrinth of quiet, oppressive anonymity, were now filled with voices of resistance. But the glow of revolution was not without its shadow. The air was thick with tension, a thin veil separating unity from chaos.

Isabella sat at the small table in the cramped safe house, her fingers tapping restlessly against the wood. Her mind was elsewhere, lost in the implications of what they had unleashed. It had been two days since the broadcast, and already Rutherford's agents were sweeping through the city, hunting down anyone associated with the resistance.

Pablo paced the room, his brows furrowed in concern. "We can't stay here much longer. The government's mobilized, and it's only a matter of time before they track us down."

"I know," Isabella replied, her voice quieter than usual. "But we can't run forever. We've exposed Rutherford's corruption. We've given people a reason to fight back. But now, we need to make sure they know how to fight."

Liberty, who had been scanning news reports on her tablet, looked up. "The media's on our side for now, but it's only a matter of time before they turn on us. They'll spin the story to fit Rutherford's narrative. We need to move fast."

Camazotz, who had remained silent until now, looked up from his position by the window. His ageless eyes were filled with both wisdom and weariness. "The world is watching, Isabella. The truth has been laid bare, but truth alone will not defeat Rutherford. Action will. You must strike where it will hurt him most."

Isabella stood up, her mind clear now. "I understand. We need to cripple his power, not just expose it."

Pablo looked between them. "You're thinking of hitting his financial networks, right? The ones we exposed in the broadcast?"

"Yes," Isabella confirmed. "But we need more than just a digital blow. We need to physically dismantle the system he's built. We need to take out his supply chains, his financial backers, the institutions that protect him."

Liberty's fingers flew across her tablet as she scanned the encrypted databases they had gained access to. "I can do that," she said, her voice firm. "I have the locations of some of his secret holdings, and I can tap into the accounts. We can pull the money from under his nose, destabilize his financial grip on the world."

"And I'll handle the muscle," Pablo said with a grin, cracking his knuckles. "We hit them hard and fast. They won't know what hit them."

Isabella nodded. "We do this together, but we have to be quick. Time is running out. The people are demanding action, and we can't give Rutherford a chance to regroup."

That night, they moved swiftly. Using the connections Liberty had cultivated and the information Camazotz had unlocked from deep within Rutherford's hidden layers, the resistance targeted key financial institutions—offshore accounts, black-market traders, and major banks that had been complicit in laundering Rutherford's wealth.

Isabella stood at the helm of their operation, guiding her team through their carefully coordinated attacks. As Liberty initiated the cyber-assault, Pablo and Camazotz infiltrated the facilities, taking out the guards and making sure no trace of their presence was left behind.

Every second mattered.

But even as the operation unfolded, the city's heart raced with unrest. Protesters clashed with police in the streets. News outlets were in full coverage mode, oscillating between condemnation and admiration for the growing resistance. Isabella could feel the pressure of their mission, but it was nothing compared to the weight of the world watching them.

As they successfully moved from target to target, the financial world began to tremble. Rutherford's empire, built on secrecy and fear, was beginning to unravel in real time. The ripple effect spread across the global economy, shaking the foundations of those who had supported Rutherford's rise to power.

Liberty grinned as the final wire was cut. "It's done," she said, tapping a few final commands into her tablet. "The funds are frozen, and we've routed the money into secure accounts. He can't touch it."

Pablo smiled grimly. "He's going to be angry."

"And desperate," Isabella added. "But desperation will make him vulnerable."

As the team gathered their things and prepared to leave, Isabella paused by the door, her hand resting on the frame. The room was silent, save for the soft hum of the city outside. They had made their mark, but the battle wasn't over. It had only just begun.

Camazotz stepped forward, his ancient eyes filled with a knowing sadness. "You've made the right move, Isabella. But there is still much to be done."

"I know," she said quietly, her voice steady but laden with determination. "We've exposed Rutherford. We've shown the world the truth. But we can't stop here. We have to ensure that the truth leads to lasting change, not just chaos."

Pablo clapped his hand on her shoulder. "We've got your back, always."

Liberty gave a small nod, her face serious. "We've started a revolution. Let's make sure we see it through."

Isabella smiled, the weight of her responsibilities shifting into something stronger—something resolute. "We will."

The next morning, news outlets reported that major financial institutions had collapsed. Stocks plummeted, and the markets were in turmoil. But amidst the chaos, there was a shift in the air—a sense that the world was no longer controlled by a single man, a single corrupt system.

And as Rutherford's empire cracked, Isabella knew they had done more than just fight back. They had ignited something greater—an unstoppable force of unity and truth. The world was waking up, and there would be no going back.

But with every revolution, there were casualties.

Rutherford would not take this lying down.

And Isabella would be ready for whatever came next.

Chapter 29: The Shadow of Retribution

The morning sun cast long shadows over the city, the once-vibrant skyline now muted beneath a clouded sky. News reports were filled with chaos: financial systems in disarray, top executives scrambling, and ordinary people suddenly aware of the deep rot that had taken hold of their world. While there was a sense of victory in the air, a creeping unease followed close behind.

Isabella sat in a dimly lit room, staring at the screen before her. The world had changed overnight, but the victory felt hollow. The ripple effects of their actions were still unfolding, and somewhere in the shadows, Rutherford was plotting his next move.

Pablo stood by the window, his eyes scanning the streets below. "It's too quiet out there," he muttered. "Too calm. It's like the calm before the storm."

Liberty, perched on a makeshift desk, was typing away furiously. "The storm's already here," she said without looking up. "Rutherford's response is fast and brutal. I've been tracking his movements, and it looks like he's consolidating his forces. He's cutting off our safehouses, shutting down our comms, and sending out agents to eliminate anyone who's connected to us."

Isabella's jaw tightened. "He's playing for keeps now."

Camazotz, who had been meditating in the corner, his ancient presence barely noticeable, now spoke. "The darkness he will unleash is vast. His thirst for power will not be quenched by financial loss alone. You must anticipate his next steps."

Isabella met his gaze, the weight of his words sinking in. "What do we do next?"

"We wait for the inevitable strike," Camazotz replied. "And then, we move."

That night, the team gathered around a map of the city, their faces drawn with exhaustion but determined. They had no illusions about their position. Their actions had exposed Rutherford's empire, but it had also made them prime targets. It was only a matter of time before the full force of his wrath would descend upon them.

Liberty had hacked into several secure systems, using her skills to stay one step ahead of Rutherford's forces. But even she was starting to run low on safe access points. "His network is tightening. I can feel it. We need to move quickly."

Pablo clenched his fists. "We've already hit him where it hurts. Financially. The people are with us now. We just need to keep pushing."

Isabella nodded but was distracted by a message flashing across the screen of her phone. It was an encrypted message, one that only someone from her past could send.

Meet me at the old church. Midnight. Alone.

It was from Hector.

Midnight came, and Isabella stood alone in the abandoned church at the edge of the city. The once-sacred space now felt like a hollow shell, the cracked windows letting in the cold night air. She had no idea what to expect. Hector had been a friend once, someone who had helped her escape before, someone who understood the stakes better than anyone. But now, everything felt different. The world had shifted beneath her feet, and she wasn't sure who she could trust anymore.

The door creaked open, and Hector stepped inside, his eyes wary and alert. He was different now—more hardened, more secretive. Isabella's heart skipped a beat as he approached.

"You came," he said, his voice low, but not without a touch of relief. "I didn't know if you would."

"Why contact me now, Hector?" Isabella asked, her eyes narrowing. "After everything that's happened?"

Hector's gaze shifted toward the door, ensuring they were alone before speaking again. "Because I've been watching Rutherford's movements. He's not just going after you. He's targeting the entire resistance, and he's using everything in his power to do it."

Isabella's stomach tightened. "What does he want from us?"

"He wants your head," Hector said bluntly. "But he also wants the Esmeralda de Tiempo."

Isabella's hand instinctively touched the pendant hidden beneath her shirt. She hadn't fully unlocked its power, but she knew it was the key to everything—everything Rutherford wanted. "He'll never get it."

"That's what I'm here to help with," Hector continued. "I know a way to neutralize him for good, but it won't be easy. It'll require more than just our team. We need to gather the right people, the right resources, and we need to strike hard before Rutherford can retaliate."

Isabella considered his words carefully. "What are you asking?"

Hector's eyes softened for a brief moment. "You've done well, Isabella. But this fight—this fight isn't just about exposing Rutherford. It's about dismantling everything he's built. The time for subtlety is over."

The next few days were a blur of preparations. Hector's plan was audacious and dangerous, but it was the only option they had left. The resistance had to take the fight directly to Rutherford, but they couldn't do it alone.

Isabella reached out to every contact they had, every ally they had made along the way. And in return, they came—some with open arms, others with distrust, but all united in one goal: to bring Rutherford down.

As the day of the final assault drew closer, Isabella found herself standing at the edge of everything she had worked for. She had lost so much already. She had sacrificed so much to get here. But the thought of the world she was fighting for—one where people like her, like her family, didn't have to live in fear—kept her going.

The night before the assault, as they gathered in their final safehouse, there was a moment of calm. They all knew what was coming, but the weight of the unknown hung heavy in the air. Liberty, usually so full of energy, sat quietly, her fingers drumming lightly on the table.

Pablo stood by the window, his arms crossed, his gaze distant.

Camazotz was meditating in the corner again, his presence a quiet anchor.

And Isabella—Isabella stood before them, as the leader of this fractured, determined team. "Tomorrow, we end this. We don't just expose Rutherford—we bring him down, for good. We finish what we started, no matter the cost."

They all nodded, a shared understanding in their eyes. No matter what came next, they would fight until the end.

Chapter 30: The Final Hour

The streets of the city were eerily quiet as the dawn broke. The usual hum of urban life was replaced with a heavy silence, as if the city itself was holding its breath. Isabella stood before her team, the weight of the upcoming battle pressing down on her shoulders. This was it—the moment they had been working toward for so long. The final showdown with Rutherford and his empire.

The sun hadn't fully risen, casting long shadows over the safehouse where they had spent their last night preparing. The room was filled with a tense energy, the team's silence reflecting the gravity of what they were about to face.

Pablo, ever the skeptic, adjusted his gear. His muscular frame was wrapped in protective armor, ready for whatever came their way. He flashed a grin at Liberty, who was adjusting the last few settings on her devices. Despite the tension, there was a spark of excitement in her eyes. The prodigy had always been eager for a challenge, and this was no different.

Camazotz stood by the window, his ageless face unreadable as he watched the city from the shadows. Despite his wisdom, even he couldn't foresee every outcome. Isabella's heart quickened as she saw him look over his shoulder at her. His gaze was heavy with meaning, but he said nothing. There was nothing more to say.

Isabella took a deep breath and looked at her team. They had all come so far—through betrayal, hardship, and loss—but now, they stood together for one final mission. This was the moment they had been preparing for, the moment that would determine the future of everything.

"It's time," she said, her voice steady. She felt the weight of the Esmeralda de Tiempo resting against her chest, its power a constant reminder of the stakes. "We take the fight to Rutherford. No more running. No more hiding."

The team nodded in unison. Liberty shut down her laptop, gathering the last of her equipment. Pablo cracked his knuckles and adjusted his tactical vest. Camazotz stepped forward, his presence commanding yet calm. "May the gods guide you," he murmured.

Isabella's gaze hardened. "And may we fight with the strength of those who came before us."

The plan was simple, but its execution would be anything but. They would strike at Rutherford's core—his main headquarters, a fortified building surrounded by layers of security and armed guards. It was the last bastion of his control. But the assault would be two-pronged. While Liberty would use her hacking skills to create distractions and breach his surveillance systems, Isabella, Pablo, and Camazotz would infiltrate the compound from the ground level. They would be the physical force, the distraction that allowed Liberty to break through the digital barriers.

Isabella knew that Rutherford would be expecting them. They had been tracking his movements for weeks, studying his patterns. But Rutherford had grown unpredictable, and there was a part of her that felt uneasy about the unknowns they were about to face. He was no fool—he had seen their success in taking down his financial empire, and now he would be ready for them.

As they neared the compound, a sense of finality hung in the air. There was no turning back. This would either be the end of Rutherford's reign or the end of their struggle altogether.

The first part of their plan was executed flawlessly. Liberty's expertise allowed them to bypass the outer security measures, her code slipping unnoticed through the cracks of Rutherford's systems. She guided them through the layers of firewalls and encryption as if she had done it a thousand times before. Every command she entered was precise, the result of years of honing her craft.

"First door is down," Liberty's voice crackled through their earpieces. "You're good to go."

Isabella signaled to the others. They moved in synchronicity, quiet but swift. The compound loomed before them, its exterior imposing, its interior a labyrinth of hallways and elevators. This was where Rutherford's empire had been built, where the strings of his power had been pulled for so long.

They navigated through the building's darkened halls, avoiding cameras and guards, their every movement calculated. Camazotz led the way, his senses sharp as ever, his presence both an asset and a mystery. He moved like a shadow, never making a sound.

Pablo and Isabella flanked him, eyes constantly scanning for danger. The tension was palpable, each step taking them closer to the confrontation that would either secure their future or destroy it entirely.

They reached the heart of the compound after what felt like hours. A reinforced steel door stood between them and Rutherford's inner sanctum. This was it—the final barrier.

Isabella turned to Liberty. "Can you get us in?"

"Already ahead of you," Liberty replied. "Give me a second."

A soft beep echoed through their earpieces, and the door clicked open.

As they stepped through, the room beyond was far larger than Isabella had anticipated. It was an expansive chamber, filled with high-tech monitors, flickering screens, and the hum of machinery that powered Rutherford's empire. At the center of the room stood a massive desk, behind which Rutherford was waiting, his back turned to them.

Isabella's heart pounded in her chest. She had prepared for this moment, but standing face to face with him—after everything he had done—felt different. It felt like fate.

Rutherford slowly turned in his chair, his cold eyes meeting hers. "I've been waiting for this," he said, his voice dripping with contempt. "You think you've won? That you can undo what's been set in motion? You have no idea what you're up against."

"We'll find out," Isabella replied, her voice steady despite the adrenaline coursing through her.

Without another word, the final battle began.

The room erupted into chaos. Guards flooded in from hidden entrances, and the air was filled with the sounds of weapons being drawn. Isabella ducked behind a column, her mind racing as she mentally coordinated with her team. Liberty was already hacking into the building's systems, disabling cameras and creating confusion among the guards.

Pablo charged forward, his strength a force of nature as he took down the first wave of attackers. Camazotz was beside him, his movements fluid and precise, as if he were a part of the very shadows themselves.

But Rutherford wasn't just a puppet master—he was a force to be reckoned with. As Isabella engaged in a fierce standoff with one of his elite guards, she heard a loud crackling sound echo through the room. Rutherford had activated something—something powerful. A force field began to rise from the floor, surrounding him and his command center.

"Not so fast," Rutherford's voice echoed through the room. "You'll never reach me now."

Isabella's heart sank. But she had come too far to let this be the end.

"Liberty," she barked into the comms. "We need to get through that barrier."

"Working on it," Liberty replied, her voice calm despite the chaos.

The battle raged on around them, but Isabella focused on the task at hand. She had come to end Rutherford's reign. Nothing—nothing—was going to stop her.

Chapter 31: Unleashing the Past

The hum of the force field vibrated through the room, its electric pulse a constant reminder of Rutherford's superiority. Isabella could feel the tension in the air, thick with the weight of the moment. The walls were closing in, and it was clear that time was running out. Liberty's voice crackled through the earpiece again, tinged with urgency.

"I'm almost in," Liberty said, her tone sharp but confident. "Just hold your position for a few more seconds."

Isabella's grip tightened around the Esmeralda de Tiempo. The stone pulsed softly beneath her fingers, as though it, too, was aware of the peril they faced. She could feel its power within her—unstable, volatile, but undeniably potent. It had been a long journey, one filled with pain, discovery, and sacrifice. But now, standing at the precipice of everything she had fought for, Isabella understood her role. The stone's power wasn't just about changing history. It was about shaping the future.

"Stay with me, Pablo," she said, motioning for her companion to stay close as they ducked behind a large pillar, narrowly avoiding the barrage of gunfire from Rutherford's guards.

Pablo grinned, his broad shoulders rising and falling with each labored breath. "You think I'm going anywhere?" His voice held the familiar confidence that Isabella had come to rely on, even in the darkest of times.

Camazotz, standing a few paces behind, was calm as ever. His presence, though silent, was a force of nature. He surveyed the battlefield with a look that seemed to see beyond the physical space around them. His eyes locked on Isabella, and for a moment, she felt an unspoken understanding pass between them.

The immortal wizard had seen this before. He knew what was coming. And for once, Isabella was certain she did, too.

A sharp metallic clink echoed from the far side of the room, snapping her out of her reverie. Liberty's voice rang out with a triumphant edge.

"Got it! The field's down, you're clear!"

Isabella didn't hesitate. "Pablo, Camazotz, now!"

In an instant, Pablo charged, his massive frame bulldozing through the remaining guards with brutal efficiency. His fists connected with flesh and bone, sending opponents sprawling as they tried to react. Camazotz followed, his movements a blur as he danced around attackers, his hands weaving magic through the air. Where his fingertips brushed, sparks flew, and the guards fell back, their weapons useless against the ancient power he wielded.

Isabella moved swiftly, ducking beneath a burst of gunfire, her heart pounding in her chest as she sprinted toward Rutherford. Every step felt heavier, the weight of the stone growing more intense with each passing moment. She couldn't afford to falter—not now.

Rutherford, his back still turned, remained seated behind his massive desk, his hands steepled in front of him. The force field was down, but his smug expression hadn't wavered. He knew the battle was far from over.

"You really think you can defeat me, Isabella?" Rutherford's voice was chilling, his tone dripping with venomous disdain. "The Esmeralda de Tiempo is nothing but a toy to me. You're out of your depth."

Isabella's breath was ragged, but she didn't slow. The stone in her hand pulsed with an energy that she could barely contain. It was as though the stone recognized her anger, her desperation. Its power surged in response to her determination.

"I'm not here for the stone, Rutherford," she shouted, her voice carrying across the room. "I'm here to end your reign. You've twisted the lives of too many, including mine."

For a moment, Rutherford's icy facade cracked. His eyes flashed with something resembling fear. He rose slowly from his chair, his long fingers curling around a hidden device on the desk. "You don't understand," he said, his voice low but menacing. "I'm not the one who's been playing with time. You've already lost."

Before Isabella could react, Rutherford slammed his hand onto the desk, and the entire room seemed to tremble. A low rumble echoed from the floor beneath them, and the walls shimmered with a strange, sickly light. Isabella's eyes widened. She had been expecting something—something dark and dangerous—but not this.

Rutherford had triggered a fail-safe.

"The stone won't save you this time," Rutherford sneered as he turned toward a control panel on the wall. "Now, you'll see the true power of the Esmeralda de Tiempo—and it will be mine to command."

The floor beneath Isabella's feet began to crack, and the room started to distort, its edges warping as if reality itself was being torn apart. The air grew thick, oppressive, as though time itself was buckling under the strain.

Isabella's pulse quickened. The Esmeralda de Tiempo was reacting, its energy flaring in her palm. She felt it surging through her, a tidal wave of power, and for the first time in her life, she knew she was the one in control.

"Not today," she whispered.

With a determined breath, Isabella held the stone out in front of her, letting its power course through her veins. The room seemed to darken, the walls bending and twisting as time itself unraveled around them. Rutherford's smug grin faltered as he realized what was happening. The power of the Esmeralda de Tiempo was no longer a mere tool—it was a force, a force she could wield as she saw fit.

"Stop!" Rutherford yelled, but his voice was drowned out by the swirling vortex that surrounded them. His hand reached out, but the power of the stone was already taking hold.

Isabella's voice rang out like a command. "You wanted control? Now you'll understand what true power is."

The stone flared bright, and the air was filled with an explosive energy as time itself shattered, splintering across the room like glass. The walls of Rutherford's empire crumbled, the dark, oppressive grip of his rule slipping away as Isabella's will took hold.

For the first time in years, Isabella was free.

Chapter 32: The Echo of Time

The room was still. The rumbling subsided, leaving only the lingering hum of the shattered space around them. Isabella stood in the center of it all, her body tense, her heart racing, the Esmeralda de Tiempo still glowing faintly in her hand. Time itself seemed to have paused, as though it was holding its breath, waiting for her next move.

Around her, the distorted walls slowly began to stabilize, but the damage was done. Rutherford's control, his empire of manipulation, had been undone. He lay motionless on the floor, his once-commanding presence now reduced to a crumpled figure. The device he had triggered lay in pieces scattered across the room.

Isabella looked down at the stone, the power that had just surged through her body still echoing in her veins. It felt both exhilarating and terrifying, the raw energy of the universe at her fingertips. But with it came a weight—one that was hard to ignore. The Esmeralda de Tiempo was more than just a tool; it was a responsibility. And that burden, now heavier than ever, was hers to bear.

"Isabella..." Camazotz's voice was soft, his presence like a comforting shadow in the room. "You've done it. The future is yours to shape now."

She didn't answer right away, her gaze fixed on the stone. It was warm against her palm, a reminder of how far she'd come and how much she still had to learn.

"Is she okay?" Pablo's voice, always a bit too loud, broke through the silence. He was standing near the door, his eyes scanning the room, his body still tense from the recent fight.

"I'm fine," Isabella said, her voice steady, though she knew the storm inside her wasn't over. Not yet.

Rutherford stirred, groaning on the floor, his hand moving feebly towards the remnants of the control panel. But it was no use. The stone had already neutralized his technology, and without it, he was just a man, powerless and defeated.

"You're finished, Rutherford," Isabella said, her voice sharp and final. "Your empire ends here."

Rutherford's eyes flickered, a brief flash of defiance crossing his face before it melted into something far darker—a bitter acceptance. "You think you've won? You've merely delayed the inevitable. The stone... its power... it's too much for you to control. You'll see. You'll all see."

Isabella clenched her jaw. She could hear the truth in his words, the seed of doubt he had planted in her mind. The power of the stone was vast, and even with her newfound strength, she felt the weight of its potential destruction.

"You're wrong," she said, her voice low but steady. "I control the stone, not the other way around."

Rutherford's lips curled into a sneer. "Do you really believe that? Time... time isn't something that can be controlled by anyone. Not even you, Isabella."

His words hung in the air like a shadow, and for a moment, Isabella felt the doubt creeping in. Could she truly control time? Could anyone?

"You don't get to decide that," she said firmly. "The future is mine to shape."

Pablo stepped forward, his broad frame casting a shadow over Rutherford. "Enough talk, Isabella. We've won. Let's move."

But Isabella didn't move. She couldn't. Not yet.

She turned her gaze to the stone again, feeling the pulse of its energy beneath her skin. The weight of what she had just done was starting to settle in, and it was overwhelming. She had used the Esmeralda de Tiempo to undo Rutherford's plans, to break his hold on time itself, but what would happen now? Would the stone keep her safe from its own power? Or was this just the beginning of a much larger storm?

"Camazotz," Isabella said, her voice quieter this time, full of uncertainty. "What if he's right? What if I can't control it?"

The wizard, standing at her side, placed a hand on her shoulder, his touch gentle yet reassuring. "No one has ever wielded the Esmeralda de Tiempo before in the way you have, Isabella. But that doesn't mean you can't. You are not defined by the stone, but by what you choose to do with it."

"But what if I make the wrong choice?" Isabella whispered, the fear that had been buried deep inside her rising to the surface.

"Fear is a part of it," Camazotz said softly. "It's a sign that you understand the power in your hands. But don't let it rule you. You are the one who decides what the stone will be. Not the other way around."

His words, though simple, were enough to ground her. The Esmeralda de Tiempo had always been part of her journey, but it didn't have to define her. She would choose its path. She would choose the future.

Pablo gave her a small grin, sensing her shift in resolve. "You heard him. Now, let's finish this. We've got a whole world to set right."

Isabella nodded, finally allowing herself to breathe. With a deep breath, she felt the stone's power recede slightly, no longer pulsing with the same intensity it had moments before. It was still there, still waiting for her command. But for now, she was in control.

Together, they left the ruined room behind, the echoes of Rutherford's defeat fading into the past. The future lay ahead, uncertain but full of possibility. Isabella could only imagine what came next, but one thing was certain: she was no longer the girl who had entered that room. She was something more, something new. The keeper of time, the guardian of the Esmeralda de Tiempo.

And this was only the beginning.

Chapter 33: The Burden of Time

The sun had long set over the horizon, casting the world in shades of deep blue and soft purples. The night air in the abandoned city felt unusually cold, and Isabella wrapped her coat tighter around her shoulders as she walked beside Camazotz. Pablo and Liberty were ahead, scouting the area for any potential threats. The group had been moving steadily, but no one had said much since they left the ruins of Rutherford's lair.

The silence between them was heavy, like the air before a storm. Isabella could feel the weight of the Esmeralda de Tiempo hanging in the small pouch at her waist, a constant reminder of the power she wielded and the danger it represented.

"You're quiet," Camazotz remarked after a long stretch of silence. His voice was calm, as always, but there was an underlying concern in his tone.

"I'm thinking," Isabella replied, her voice distant.

"About Rutherford?" Camazotz asked.

"Not just him," she said, pausing for a moment as she stared at the path ahead. "What happens now? The stone, its power… It's too much. I can feel it every time I hold it. It's like it's calling to me, asking for something I don't fully understand."

Camazotz studied her carefully. "The stone has always chosen its keeper," he said. "It chose you, Isabella. That means you are ready for what it holds. But that doesn't mean it will be easy. You must accept its power, not fight it."

Isabella shook her head, frustration building in her chest. "I don't want to control time. I don't want to be responsible for—" She faltered, not quite sure how to express the fears that were now consuming her.

"You fear losing control," Camazotz finished for her, his words cutting through her thoughts. "But control is an illusion, Isabella. You can only guide it, not tame it. The stone does not belong to you—it is a force of the universe itself. Your role is to wield it with wisdom and balance."

"And what if I fail?" she asked, her voice barely a whisper.

Camazotz was silent for a moment before answering. "Failure is a part of learning. What matters is how you rise from it. Time itself is not a chain—it is a river, always flowing, always shifting. It cannot be stopped. Only the way you navigate it will define your future."

Isabella processed his words, but the weight of the stone still felt unbearable. It was not just a tool for time travel—it was more than that. She had felt its power surge through her when she defeated Rutherford, but each time she tapped into it, she felt like she was standing on the edge of an abyss. And no matter how much she tried to steady herself, it was there, a chasm of uncertainty.

"You think I'm ready for this?" Isabella asked, her voice quieter now, as if she was unsure whether she was asking Camazotz or herself.

"I know you are," he said with certainty. "You have been shaped by everything you've gone through. The stone doesn't choose recklessly. It chose you for a reason."

"But I don't understand the reason," she confessed. "I still don't know what it wants from me."

"Perhaps," Camazotz said thoughtfully, "the stone doesn't want anything from you. Perhaps it simply exists, and it is up to you to decide what to do with it."

Isabella looked up at the darkening sky, her eyes distant. She had always thought of herself as an ordinary person, someone simply trying to survive in a world that seemed to bend and twist under the weight of circumstances beyond her control. But now? Now, she was a keeper of time itself.

"You're right," she said quietly. "I have to figure out what to do with it."

As the group continued walking, the world around them seemed eerily still. There was no movement, no sign of life in the decaying city, and Isabella couldn't shake the feeling that they were being watched. She glanced around, but there was nothing but the cold night.

Liberty came rushing back, her face flushed with excitement. "I found something!" she exclaimed. "Not far from here. It looks like an old temple, buried under the rubble. There are symbols on the walls—ancient ones. It could be another clue about the stone's origins."

Isabella's heart quickened. They had been searching for answers ever since they'd left Rutherford's stronghold, trying to piece together the history of the Esmeralda de Tiempo and its connection to the world. Every step felt like it brought them closer to a greater understanding, yet each discovery only raised more questions.

"Lead the way," Isabella said, her voice resolute, despite the uncertainty gnawing at her.

They followed Liberty through the ruins, the air thick with dust and the weight of history. As they approached the site, Isabella felt a strange hum beneath her feet, a vibration that seemed to echo through the very ground they walked on. The stones beneath her boots felt alive, pulsing with energy.

They reached the entrance of the temple, half-hidden by rubble. The door was engraved with intricate symbols—symbols that Isabella immediately recognized. They were similar to the ones she had seen in the visions the Esmeralda de Tiempo had shown her. The symbols of time.

"This is it," Isabella murmured. "This is where it all began."

The group stepped inside, their footsteps echoing in the vast, hollow space. The walls were lined with more symbols, more intricate carvings that seemed to move as they gazed upon them. The air was thick with the sense of something ancient, something powerful. The Esmeralda de Tiempo pulsed again, as if reacting to the environment around them.

Pablo glanced around, his eyes narrowed in suspicion. "This place… it doesn't feel right."

Isabella could feel it too. The air felt charged, heavy with an unseen presence. The stone at her side seemed to hum in anticipation, as if calling to something hidden deep within the temple.

"Stay close," she said, her voice firm. "We don't know what we're dealing with here."

They ventured deeper into the temple, the walls narrowing as they moved further in. Soon, they reached the heart of the structure—a large chamber that seemed to pulse with energy. In the center stood an altar, a pedestal bathed in the faint glow of moonlight filtering through cracks in the stone ceiling. And upon that pedestal was a stone—a smaller, yet strikingly familiar stone.

It was identical to the Esmeralda de Tiempo, yet different. Darker. More worn, as if it had been in existence far longer than any of them could fathom.

Isabella's breath caught in her throat. "The origin," she whispered. "This is where it began."

The moment she stepped forward, the ground trembled, and the air grew thick with an unnatural force. The stone on the pedestal began to glow, and for the first time since taking the Esmeralda de Tiempo into her hands, Isabella felt truly out of her depth.

Something was stirring. Something ancient.

And it was awakening.

Chapter 34: The Awakening

The stone on the pedestal pulsated, a dark, almost sinister glow that illuminated the chamber in eerie shadows. The air grew heavy with a force that pressed down on Isabella, as if the very walls were alive, closing in around them. She could feel her pulse quicken, the Esmeralda de Tiempo at her side thrumming in response, as though reacting to the presence of its twin.

"Isabella, don't touch it," Camazotz warned, his voice low and grave.

But it was too late. The pull of the stone was undeniable, a magnetic force drawing her closer, urging her to understand its power. The symbols carved into the walls flared to life, glowing with the same dark energy emanating from the stone. A low hum resonated in the chamber, vibrating in her bones.

"What is this?" Liberty whispered, her voice tinged with awe and fear. "What do we do?"

Isabella's hand trembled as she reached toward the stone. She didn't know what compelled her, whether it was the Esmeralda de Tiempo calling to it or something deeper, something ancient. The instant her fingers brushed the cool surface, a shockwave of energy rippled through her, knocking her back. Her head spun, and the world seemed to stretch, distort, as if time itself was fracturing.

She gasped for air, struggling to steady herself, her body trembling as the force within the chamber surged. The glow of the two stones intensified, intertwining in a blinding flash. For a moment, everything went white, and Isabella felt herself falling, falling into a void of swirling shadows.

When the light faded, she found herself standing in the center of a vast, empty expanse. The air was thick with the smell of earth and decay, the ground cracked beneath her boots. There were no walls here, no ceiling, just an infinite horizon of nothingness. A place outside of time.

"Isabella…" The voice echoed from all directions, deep and ancient, sending chills down her spine. It was neither male nor female, neither human nor divine. It was the voice of something far older.

"Who are you?" she demanded, her voice trembling but firm. Her heart pounded in her chest, the Esmeralda de Tiempo humming faintly at her side, as though it recognized this place. "What is this place?"

"You already know," the voice replied, as if amused. "You are here because you were chosen."

A figure materialized before her, its form shifting in the void. It was neither human nor beast, its shape a fluid mass of shadows and light. Eyes—no, orbs—glowed from within its form, and a sense of vast, unfathomable power radiated from it.

"You are the keeper of the Esmeralda de Tiempo," the voice continued. "But you have yet to understand its true nature."

Isabella swallowed hard, trying to gather her strength. "What do you mean? The stone… it's a tool for time travel, isn't it? Why are you telling me this?"

The figure's orbs of light narrowed, and Isabella felt the weight of its gaze pierce her very soul. "The Esmeralda de Tiempo is not simply a tool. It is a fragment of the universe itself, a shard of the First Hour, when time and space were born. It holds the power to shape reality, to create and destroy. But it is not the only one."

Isabella's blood ran cold. "What do you mean, 'not the only one'?"

The figure's form flickered, and then, with a terrible stillness, it spoke again. "The stone you found—the one you hold—is the key. But the other, the one you saw in the temple, is its counterpart. Together, they govern the balance of time. One stone holds creation. The other, destruction."

The words hung in the air like an omen, and Isabella felt a chill seep into her bones.

"But I don't want that responsibility," she whispered. "I didn't ask for any of this."

The figure's orbs dimmed, and for a moment, there was silence. Then it spoke, its voice as ancient and inevitable as time itself.

"The stones are not yours to refuse. They were always meant to be in your hands. You must understand: the balance of time is fragile. It is now in your power to restore it—or to break it."

A sharp pain lanced through Isabella's head, and she gasped, clutching her temples as flashes of images filled her mind—fractured timelines, worlds burning, the lives of countless people crumbling. The two stones, the Esmeralda de Tiempo and its counterpart, swirling together, creating something new, something powerful.

"No!" she cried out, trying to shut out the visions. "I can't do this! I'm not ready."

The figure's form flickered again, and it reached out, not physically, but through the very fabric of space, its presence surrounding Isabella, pressing against her. "You do not have a choice. The stones are not bound by your will. They are bound by fate."

A blinding light exploded around her, and for a second, Isabella felt as if she were being torn apart by the force. The next thing she knew, she was back in the temple, gasping for air, the weight of the Esmeralda de Tiempo pressing against her chest.

She staggered back, her heart pounding in her chest, and her mind spinning with the implications of what she had just learned. The other stone. The counterpart. Creation and destruction. She had only just begun to grasp the enormity of what was at stake.

"Isabella!" Liberty's voice broke through the haze, and she rushed to her side, grabbing her arm to steady her.

Pablo and Camazotz were close behind, their eyes wide with concern. "What happened?" Pablo asked, his voice tinged with panic. "You just—"

"I saw it," Isabella whispered, her voice strained. "The other stone. The one that controls destruction. It's part of the balance. Creation and destruction. Together, they shape time."

Camazotz's expression darkened as he stepped closer. "You were not meant to see that," he said quietly, his voice heavy with warning. "The stones have a way of revealing themselves, but you must resist the temptation to seek the other. It will corrupt you, Isabella. I've seen it happen before."

Isabella looked down at the Esmeralda de Tiempo, the stone glowing faintly at her waist. She could still feel the hum of its power, and it was more than she could bear. The burden of it all felt like an insurmountable weight pressing against her chest.

"But I don't know what to do," she whispered, her voice filled with uncertainty. "How do I stop this from destroying everything?"

Camazotz met her gaze, his expression somber. "You cannot stop it alone. We must find the other stone before Rutherford does. He will stop at nothing to use it to shape the world to his will."

Liberty clenched her fists, determination flickering in her eyes. "Then let's find it. Before it's too late."

Isabella nodded, the fire of resolve burning in her chest, but she knew the path ahead would not be easy. The stones were not just tools. They were forces of the universe itself. Forces that could break everything they had fought for—or reshape it in ways they could never imagine.

The true test was just beginning.

Chapter 35: The Hunt for the Other Stone

The chill of the night air settled over the ancient city like a heavy cloak, the moonlight reflecting off the crumbled ruins of what had once been a mighty civilization. The streets were eerily quiet, the only sounds the distant calls of night birds and the soft rustling of leaves in the wind. Isabella stood on the edge of the old temple, her heart pounding as she gazed out into the darkened city.

She could feel it. The pull of the Esmeralda de Tiempo, a magnetic force that drew her to something—something important—just out of reach. The ancient stone hummed faintly at her side, its power flickering like a heartbeat.

"You feel it too, don't you?" Camazotz's voice cut through the silence, and Isabella turned to find him standing just behind her, his ageless eyes watching her intently.

She nodded. "I don't know what it is, but it's like the stone's calling to me. It's guiding me, or maybe… warning me."

"It is both," Camazotz replied, his voice heavy with an ancient weight. "The Esmeralda de Tiempo is not a mere artifact. It is a vessel of time itself, holding within it the potential to shape the very fabric of reality. And the other stone—the counterpart—it is just as powerful. Together, they can destroy or rebuild time, but only if they are in the right hands."

Isabella swallowed hard. "I have to find it, don't I?"

Camazotz didn't answer immediately, his gaze distant, as if lost in thought. When he finally spoke, his voice was quieter, almost regretful. "You will. But it will not be easy. The stone calls to those with a purpose, but it also draws the unwanted. There are forces who will stop at nothing to claim it."

"Rutherford," she muttered, clenching her fists. His name was like a curse on her lips. Judge Malcolm Rutherford, the man who had destroyed so many lives—her own included. He was obsessed with control, and he had already proven that he would do anything to seize power, even if it meant altering time itself.

"He will come for you," Camazotz warned. "He's already sensed the presence of the other stone. And when he finds it…" He trailed off, letting the implication hang in the air.

"We can't let that happen," Liberty said from behind them, her sharp voice breaking through the tension. Isabella turned to see Liberty, her youthful face filled with determination, her eyes gleaming with the fire of someone ready to fight. "We have to stop him. We have to get to it first."

Isabella felt a surge of gratitude toward Liberty. The young prodigy had been by her side through every twist and turn, her unwavering loyalty and brilliance a lifeline in the midst of all the chaos. "I know. But we can't just go charging in blindly. Rutherford's not the only threat we're facing."

Pablo stepped forward, his massive frame cutting a shadow in the dim light. "What's our plan, then?" His voice was rough but resolute. "We can't wait around while Rutherford catches up. We need to take action. We need to find the other stone before he does."

Isabella felt a pang of doubt, but she pushed it aside. She had never been a leader. She had never been someone to guide others. But now, with the weight of the Esmeralda de Tiempo in her hands, she had no choice but to rise to the occasion. The fate of the world, of time itself, depended on it.

"Camazotz, do you know where the other stone is?" Isabella asked, her voice firm, her gaze unwavering.

Camazotz looked at her, his ancient eyes filled with the wisdom of millennia. "I do," he said softly. "But it is not a place that can be easily found. It is hidden in a place outside of time, a nexus where the past, present, and future intersect. It is a place of great power, but also of great danger."

Isabella took a deep breath, steeling herself for what lay ahead. "Then we'll go there. We'll find the stone before Rutherford does."

"We will need to travel through time again," Camazotz added. "To the nexus."

Liberty's eyes widened. "How will we get there?"

"We will use the Esmeralda de Tiempo," Camazotz replied. "But it will not be easy. The journey will be perilous, and we will be vulnerable to the forces that guard the nexus."

Isabella nodded, feeling the weight of responsibility settle over her once more. "Then let's get ready. We don't have time to waste."

Hours later, the group gathered in the heart of the ancient ruins, the moon now high in the sky. Isabella held the Esmeralda de Tiempo tightly, feeling its power surge beneath her fingertips. She closed her eyes, focusing on the pull of the stone, the way it seemed to beckon her toward something far beyond the world they knew.

"We must prepare ourselves for what lies ahead," Camazotz warned as he stepped to her side, his voice serious. "The nexus is a place where time collapses upon itself. It is a realm where the very rules of existence are twisted, and the boundaries between past, present, and future blur. You must be ready for anything."

Isabella nodded, feeling the weight of the task ahead. She couldn't afford to hesitate. The fate of not just her world, but countless others, was riding on her shoulders.

She took a deep breath, summoning the courage to take the first step toward the unknown.

With the Esmeralda de Tiempo in hand, Isabella and her companions stepped forward, the air around them shimmering with the power of the stone.

In an instant, the world around them dissolved into a vortex of light and shadow, the fabric of time itself twisting and warping as they were pulled into the very heart of the nexus.

Chapter 36: The Nexus of Time

The moment they crossed the threshold of the nexus, everything changed.

The world around them shattered, not like glass, but more like the smooth surface of a pond disturbed by a single drop of water. Reality itself seemed to warp, twisting into shapes that defied comprehension. Time, space, and light flickered like distant stars. The air was thick, heavy with the weight of centuries, the pressure of countless moments crammed into an impossible space.

Isabella blinked, trying to steady herself, but it was as if her body didn't know where to be. One second she was standing in the ruins of the ancient city, and the next, she was weightless, suspended in an expanse that had no beginning or end. Her heart raced in her chest as she reached out, feeling for something, anything to anchor herself.

"Stay close," Camazotz's voice echoed, though she couldn't tell where it was coming from. "This place is dangerous. Time does not move here as it does in your world."

Isabella's feet found solid ground once again, but the sensation was disorienting. The ground beneath her was smooth and reflective, like dark glass, yet it stretched into infinity. There was no sky, no horizon—just a swirling mass of colors and lights that flickered in and out of existence. It felt like the edges of every timeline, every memory, converging in one place.

Liberty's voice came from somewhere behind her. "This is... impossible."

"I know," Isabella replied, taking a step forward. "But we have no choice. We have to keep going."

Pablo grunted, his footsteps heavy as they echoed in the vast emptiness. "Where do we go? This place doesn't exactly have road signs."

"Follow the pull of the stone," Camazotz said, his presence a steady guide in the chaos. "The Esmeralda de Tiempo knows the way. It will lead us to the other stone."

Isabella gripped the stone tighter, feeling the hum of its energy under her skin. There was something ancient and familiar about it, but at the same time, the power it radiated felt alien, distant. It felt like an echo of something long lost—something she was only beginning to understand.

"Do you feel it?" Liberty asked, her voice low but full of awe. "The way it pulls at you... like it's... alive."

"I do," Isabella answered, nodding. The stone was calling her, urging her onward. But there was something else, too. Something darker, lurking just beneath the surface of its power. A warning. She couldn't shake the feeling that they were being watched.

"This way," Camazotz said, pointing toward a distant, shifting glow that pulsed in the far reaches of the nexus. "That is where we must go. But be cautious. The nexus is not a place for the unprepared."

As they moved toward the light, the landscape around them shifted. It was as if they were passing through multiple realities at once— glimpses of different times and places flashing by in an endless stream. They saw visions of ancient civilizations, of battles fought in the dust of forgotten cities, of future worlds where technology had surpassed the human soul. Each vision was fleeting, yet vivid enough to leave an impression on their minds.

Isabella's heart skipped a beat as she caught sight of something in the corner of her vision—a shadow moving through the shifting currents of time. For a brief moment, she thought she saw the outline of someone she knew, someone from her past. But before she could focus on it, the image was gone, replaced by another, and then another.

"Focus," Camazotz's voice cut through her thoughts. "You must not let yourself be distracted. The nexus will use your memories against you, twisting them into illusions. Do not lose yourself in what you see."

Isabella nodded, forcing herself to stay grounded in the present. She couldn't afford to be distracted, not now. Not when they were so close.

But as they continued to move, the pressure in the air grew heavier. The stone in her hand pulsed more urgently, and the sound of distant whispers began to echo through the nexus, a cacophony of voices speaking in languages she didn't understand. Some were familiar, the faintest echoes of people she had known, their voices laced with fear and desperation.

And then she heard it.

A voice that sent a chill down her spine.

"Isabella."

She froze, her blood running cold. It was a voice she had heard once, long ago. A voice from her past, a voice that should have stayed buried.

"Isabella…" the voice repeated, louder this time, and she felt the ground beneath her tremble.

"Don't listen to it," Camazotz warned, his eyes narrowing. "It is a trick. The nexus will exploit your weaknesses, your doubts. Keep moving."

But Isabella couldn't move. She stood frozen, staring into the dark, her heart racing. The voice—it was her mother's voice. But her mother was gone, lost to the very system that had forced Isabella to live in the shadows. This couldn't be real.

"Isabella, please…" The voice grew softer, more pleading. "Come back to me…"

The ground beneath her cracked, and a cold wind blew through the nexus, carrying with it the scent of familiar flowers from her childhood. Isabella's hands shook, the stone in her palm now burning hot. The pull was stronger than ever, but the voice... it held her in place.

Suddenly, she felt a hand on her shoulder. It was Pablo, his grip firm, pulling her away from the illusion.

"Don't get lost in this," he muttered, his voice low and steady. "We've got a job to do."

Isabella blinked, the vision of her mother fading. Her breath came in short gasps, and for a moment, she felt dizzy. The weight of the nexus threatened to swallow her whole.

"I'm… I'm okay," she whispered, shaking her head. "I just... I just need to focus."

"Let's go," Camazotz urged. "The stone is close."

They moved forward again, and the shadows in the distance seemed to stretch toward them, like dark tendrils reaching out from the fabric of time. The closer they got to the glowing light, the more distorted the world around them became. Time seemed to slow, and then, without warning, it sped up again. Past, present, and future collided in a dizzying blur.

And then, they arrived.

Before them stood a massive, ancient door, its surface covered in intricate carvings that pulsed with the same light as the stone in Isabella's hand. The Esmeralda de Tiempo hummed, vibrating with energy as if it recognized its twin.

"This is it," Camazotz said, his voice reverberating in the heavy air. "The other stone lies beyond this door."

Isabella stepped forward, her pulse racing as the door slowly began to open, revealing a blinding light from within.

The nexus was about to reveal its greatest secret. But Isabella knew—nothing would come easy. The true test was only just beginning.

Chapter 37: The Heart of the Nexus

The door creaked open, the sound echoing through the shifting, timeless void around them. The light that poured from within was blinding, pure, and unyielding. It felt as though it were not just light, but the essence of time itself—an eternal force, the pulse of every moment that had ever existed.

Isabella hesitated at the threshold, feeling the weight of the decision before her. She glanced back at her companions, their faces reflecting the same uncertainty, the same fear.

"This is it," Camazotz said, his voice steady, though there was a flicker of something ancient in his eyes—something that spoke of deep, unspoken knowledge. "Beyond this door lies the heart of the nexus, the true power of the Esmeralda de Tiempo. But remember—time is not something to be controlled without consequence."

"I'm ready," Isabella said, though her voice trembled. Her grip on the Esmeralda tightened. The stone hummed against her skin, its power resonating with the very core of her being. She could feel its call, its pull, urging her forward, guiding her toward destiny.

But that pull was not without a cost. Every step she took toward the door felt like a weight pressing on her chest, as though the very fabric of reality was trying to hold her back.

"I've spent my life running from things I couldn't control," she whispered, mostly to herself. "Now I have the chance to change everything. I won't turn back."

Liberty, who had been unusually quiet, stepped up beside her. "Isabella, we've all sacrificed so much to get here. We can't let it be for nothing."

Pablo, ever the protector, grunted and crossed his arms. "We're in this together. No matter what happens next, we face it as a team."

Isabella nodded, taking in the words of her friends. They had come this far, endured so much, and there was no turning back now. The door was wide enough for them to pass through, but it felt like a threshold between worlds—between what was and what could be.

Taking a deep breath, she stepped forward, into the blinding light.

As she crossed the threshold, the world around her warped once again. She felt her body stretching, bending through layers of time— past, present, and future swirling around her like fragmented memories. The air grew thick, and the ground beneath her felt unstable, shifting with every movement. It was as though she was walking between moments, each one unstable, each one fighting against her passage.

Then, just as quickly as it had begun, everything stopped. The light vanished, leaving behind a vast, silent expanse—an infinite, ever-shifting plain, like the inside of a living, breathing clock. Time itself seemed to pulse in the air, swirling around her, becoming a tangible force.

And there, in the center of the expanse, was the source of the power—the other stone. The Esmeralda de Memento. It sat upon an altar, glowing with an ethereal light that seemed to draw every particle of time toward it. The stone was large, unlike the Esmeralda de Tiempo, but its energy was just as undeniable. Where the

Esmeralda de Tiempo thrummed with potential, the Esmeralda de Memento radiated the feeling of loss, of forgotten things, of what could never be reclaimed.

Isabella took a hesitant step toward it, and as she did, the space around her trembled. The moment her foot touched the ground, a voice filled the air, its sound deep and resonant, like it came from the very center of time itself.

"Why do you seek to change the course of history, child of the present?"

The voice was both familiar and alien, like a memory she couldn't quite place. She spun around, searching for its source, but there was no one in sight. The words felt like they were coming from everywhere and nowhere at once.

"I seek to protect the future," Isabella said, her voice steady despite the rising fear in her chest. "I want to give people like me—people who are forgotten—what they deserve. A chance. A voice. A life."

"And what makes you worthy of such power?" The voice asked, its tone not accusing but probing, like it sought to understand her very essence.

"I've fought for it," Isabella replied, her grip tightening around the Esmeralda de Tiempo. "I've fought for my survival. For my community. For my future. I've paid the price of everything I've lost to get here. And I won't let fear control me anymore."

For a long moment, there was silence. Isabella could feel the weight of the voice's scrutiny, its search for truth. The light around her flickered, as though the stone itself was considering her words. Finally, it spoke again.

"You speak of the future, but you do not understand the price. The Esmeralda de Memento does not just change the future—it alters the past. It erases what has already been written. Once you touch it, you cannot return to what was."

Isabella stepped closer to the altar, ignoring the rising unease in her chest. "I'm not afraid of what I can't control. I'm ready to face the consequences."

The air around her seemed to pulse with energy, and the stone on the altar flickered with life, drawing her closer, its call irresistible. She reached out, her fingers brushing against the surface, and in that instant, a wave of power surged through her.

Time itself seemed to collapse, folding in on itself. She saw flashes of her own life—her family, the streets of Chronic Bay, the day she had first discovered the Esmeralda de Tiempo. And then, she saw something else. A dark figure, hidden in the shadows of history, pulling the strings of power, manipulating events from behind the scenes.

Her breath caught as she recognized him—the face was older, more weathered, but there was no mistaking it. Judge Malcolm Rutherford.

The stone's power surged again, and Isabella was thrown backward, her body colliding with the hard surface of the ground. The vision of Rutherford faded, but the fear it left in her lingered.

"We must leave," Camazotz's voice broke through her panic. "This place is not meant for mortals. It will tear you apart if you remain too long."

Isabella pushed herself to her feet, her heart racing. She could still feel the pull of the stone, the temptation to claim its power. But she knew now—she couldn't let herself be consumed by it. Not yet. Not until she had the answers she needed.

Pablo and Liberty rushed to her side, pulling her away from the altar. "Isabella, we have to go. The longer we stay, the more it'll affect us."

Isabella nodded, shaking her head to clear the lingering haze. She had almost given in, almost lost herself. But she could feel the weight of the stone still in her hand, and she knew—this was not the end of the journey. It was only the beginning.

As they retreated, the nexus shifted once more, the world around them crumbling back into the endless expanse of light and shadow.

The real battle was about to begin.

Chapter 38: Echoes of the Past

The air was thick with the hum of time itself as Isabella and her companions stumbled back through the door they had entered. The moment they crossed the threshold, the world around them flickered, shifting and distorting like the tail end of a dream.

For a few moments, they were disoriented, their senses overwhelmed by the violent push and pull of temporal energy. But soon, the world stabilized, and they found themselves standing in the middle of a forgotten city—its streets eerily quiet, its buildings worn and weathered by the ravages of time.

"Where are we?" Liberty asked, her voice low and cautious. She adjusted the straps of her backpack, eyes darting around. "This doesn't look like any place I recognize."

Isabella scanned the environment, trying to place the unfamiliar surroundings. The architecture was old, but there was something distinctly timeless about the city—like it was frozen in a moment of history that never quite passed. The buildings had a mixture of ancient and modern design, cobbled streets beside gleaming metal structures that should have been centuries apart.

"We're not in the same place," Camazotz said quietly, his eyes narrowed as he took in their surroundings. He had an aura of ancient knowledge, as if he could sense things beyond mere sight. "This is not just another place in time. We've entered a nexus point—a convergence of multiple realities, stretching across history."

The words struck Isabella like a punch to the gut. The nexus, the heart of time, was not just a place of power—it was a place where realities collided, where past, present, and future coexisted in a tangled web of possibility. And in that moment, she realized they were no longer simply battling for control over the Esmeralda de Tiempo. They were fighting for control over the very fabric of existence.

"We need to move quickly," Pablo urged, his voice a steady anchor amidst the rising tension. "Before something notices we're here."

Isabella nodded, her gaze falling on the path ahead. She could feel the weight of the Esmeralda de Tiempo in her hand, its hum resonating deep in her chest. The connection to the stone was stronger than ever, as if it had sensed the shift in reality itself.

But she also felt the presence of something else. Something darker.

A shadow crossed the street ahead of them, lingering at the edge of their vision. It was no mere trick of the light. The figure was real, its form fleeting but unmistakably malevolent. It was a presence that chilled her to the core—a reminder of everything they had come here to stop.

"Do you see that?" Isabella whispered, her voice barely audible.

The others turned in unison, following her gaze. There, at the end of the street, was a figure cloaked in shadows, its face obscured by a hood. It stood motionless, watching them with an intensity that seemed to pierce through time itself.

Before anyone could react, the figure moved, gliding toward them with unnatural speed. Isabella's breath caught in her throat as it drew closer, its movements fluid and predatory.

"This is a trap," Camazotz murmured, his voice laced with urgency. "We've crossed into the heart of the storm."

Isabella instinctively stepped forward, her hand instinctively gripping the Esmeralda de Tiempo. She could feel its power swirling around her, ready to be unleashed.

But before she could act, the figure stopped in its tracks, its gaze fixed squarely on her. The air grew cold, and the stone in her hand began to pulse with an unsettling rhythm.

"Isabella Monteverdi," the figure's voice echoed, deep and hollow. "I've been waiting for you."

Isabella's heart skipped a beat. The voice—though distorted—was unmistakable. It was Judge Malcolm Rutherford.

She gritted her teeth, stepping into a defensive stance. "What do you want, Rutherford?"

The figure laughed, the sound like gravel scraping against metal. "I want what you've been running from, what you've been fighting to protect. Power. Control. The Esmeralda de Tiempo belongs to me. And you, Isabella, are merely a pawn in a game much older than you can comprehend."

The world around them seemed to darken, the atmosphere thickening with a sense of dread. Isabella could feel the stone in her hand reacting, as if it understood the threat before her. It began to vibrate, its light flickering like a heartbeat, resonating with the tension in the air.

"You're wrong," Isabella said, her voice gaining strength. "The stone doesn't belong to you. It belongs to those who fight for a future, for a chance at something better."

Rutherford's figure tilted its head, a mocking smile crossing its face. "You think you have control, don't you? But in the end, you're just another tool. Just like everyone else who's ever tried to wield power. You cannot defeat time, Isabella. Time is the ultimate master."

Before she could respond, the ground beneath them trembled, sending vibrations through their bodies. The shadowy figure of Rutherford began to dissolve, his form twisting and warping like smoke in the wind. But his voice remained, echoing through the space, resonating with an eerie finality.

"This is only the beginning. The Nexus will bend to me. The Esmeralda de Memento will be mine, and then I will rewrite history itself."

And then, just as suddenly as it had appeared, the figure was gone, leaving only the sound of distant winds howling through the crumbling city.

Isabella stood frozen, her heart pounding in her chest. The presence of Rutherford lingered in the air, a reminder of the threat they faced—one that was far greater than she had anticipated.

"We're not safe here," Camazotz said, his tone grave. "The nexus is unstable. The more you use the stone, the more it will draw him to us."

"I don't care," Isabella said, her voice fierce. "I won't let him take the stone. I won't let him take everything we've fought for."

The others exchanged worried glances, but they all nodded in agreement. They had come too far to turn back now.

"We'll need to move fast," Liberty said, adjusting the straps of her bag once again. "We need to find out where we are, and how to stop Rutherford before it's too late."

With determination in their eyes, the group set off, stepping into the strange, fragmented city that lay before them. Time, as they knew it, was breaking apart—and only by understanding the nexus, and the true power of the Esmeralda, could they hope to stop the chaos from spreading.

But as they moved deeper into the heart of the city, Isabella couldn't shake the feeling that Rutherford's shadow was already one step ahead, waiting for them in the ruins of history.

Chapter 39: The Shattered City

The city was alive in ways that were impossible to explain. It wasn't just a place; it was a reflection of time itself, a fractured mirror of countless histories overlapping and distorting, blending together into one chaotic existence. Every corner they turned revealed another contradiction: ancient ruins nestled beside futuristic towers, centuries-old markets hawking futuristic technology, and quiet, empty alleys that seemed to exist out of sync with the world around them.

"I don't like this," Pablo muttered, glancing nervously over his shoulder as they made their way through the twisting streets. His muscled form tensed, always ready for a fight, but there was no immediate danger in sight. Not yet.

Liberty walked at the front of the group, her keen eyes scanning the surroundings for any sign of a way forward. "The energy here is off. The stone is reacting differently too," she said, voice tinged with concern. Her fingers lightly brushed the tablet in her bag, her expression distant. "I think we're being pulled toward something."

Isabella felt it too—the pull, a subtle force that tugged at her chest as though the Esmeralda de Tiempo was calling her, drawing her deeper into the city's heart. The stone vibrated in her palm, its hum growing louder the farther they ventured into the labyrinthine streets. She could feel the weight of its power pressing against her, like a tide threatening to sweep her under.

"Let's keep moving," Isabella said, her voice steady but her mind racing. "We're not getting anywhere standing still."

The group moved onward, their footsteps echoing through the narrow, crumbling streets. Camazotz moved silently beside them, his ancient senses alert to every subtle shift in the air. His sharp eyes scanned every corner, every shadow, waiting for any sign of danger.

"This city doesn't belong in the timeline," he murmured, voice carrying the weight of someone who had seen too much history to be fooled by illusions. "It's a paradox, a collision of eras. If we're not careful, we could become lost here."

"Lost?" Liberty raised an eyebrow. "What do you mean by that?"

"The nexus is unstable," Camazotz replied. "Time here isn't linear. It's like walking through the cracks between worlds. There are no guarantees. One wrong step and you could find yourself stranded in a reality where nothing makes sense."

Isabella shivered at the thought. They had already been through enough. The last thing they needed was to become lost in a fractured timeline, a world where the past, present, and future bled together uncontrollably.

As they moved deeper into the city, the streets became more desolate. The air grew heavier, and the once-distant hum of the Esmeralda de Tiempo became almost unbearable. The stone pulsed in her hand like a second heartbeat, louder, faster—urgently.

Without warning, the sound of clanging metal reached their ears, followed by voices. The group stopped in their tracks, freezing at the sound of approaching footsteps. The city had been eerily silent up until this point. But now, there was movement—movement they hadn't expected.

"What was that?" Pablo asked, his hand instinctively going to the knife at his belt.

Before anyone could respond, a group of figures appeared at the end of the street. They moved with an unnatural grace, cloaked in dark robes that blended seamlessly with the shadows. Their faces were obscured, but their presence radiated an aura of coldness, of something deeply wrong.

Isabella's grip on the Esmeralda de Tiempo tightened. She didn't have to ask who they were.

"The Keepers," Camazotz said quietly, his voice carrying a weight of ancient recognition. "They are the guardians of the Nexus. They exist to preserve the balance between timelines. And they do not take kindly to intruders."

The Keepers halted in front of them, their dark hoods shifting slightly as they tilted their heads, as if assessing the group. For a long, tense moment, no one moved. The air felt thick with anticipation, like a storm was building, ready to unleash itself.

Finally, one of the figures spoke, its voice hollow and unfeeling. "You do not belong here. The stone you carry disrupts the balance. Leave now, or face the consequences."

Isabella felt her heart quicken. These were no ordinary guardians. These were ancient beings, tied to the fabric of time itself, and they weren't going to let her or her friends walk away without a fight.

"We're not here to disrupt anything," Isabella said, stepping forward. "We need the Esmeralda de Tiempo to stop someone from destroying the timeline. You have to understand. If we don't act, everything will be lost."

The Keeper who had spoken remained still, its hollow gaze fixed on Isabella. "The stone was never meant to be wielded by mortals. It is beyond your comprehension. Its power is too great for anyone to control. The Nexus will not allow it."

Isabella shook her head, frustration bubbling up inside her. "We're not trying to control it. We're trying to protect it from someone who wants to twist time for his own gain. He's already caused irreparable damage to the timeline. You have to help us stop him."

Another Keeper stepped forward, its voice low and cold. "We are the guardians of time. We do not interfere with the choices of mortals. The balance will correct itself. If you choose to continue your path, you will face the consequences."

The atmosphere around them thickened, the air growing colder. Isabella could feel the weight of the stone in her hand, its power pressing down on her. She was close to understanding its true purpose—close to unlocking its potential—but the Keepers stood in her way. She knew that to go forward, she would have to challenge them.

"We don't have time to argue," Isabella said, her voice hardening. "We will do whatever it takes to stop Rutherford, even if it means breaking the rules."

At her words, the Keepers stirred, their forms flickering like mirages. One of them raised its hand, and suddenly, the world around them began to shift again. The ground trembled beneath their feet, the city's crumbling buildings swaying as if the very fabric of reality was being torn apart.

"Then you will face the consequences of your choices," the Keeper intoned, and the ground beneath them shattered, sending the group tumbling into the unknown.

Chapter 40: Through the Cracks of Time

The world dissolved into a spiral of light and shadow.

Isabella tumbled through the void, her scream swallowed by the roaring winds of fractured time. She clutched the Esmeralda de Tiempo with all her strength, its emerald glow the only constant in the chaos. Around her, glimpses of other timelines flickered like broken film—some beautiful, others horrifying. She caught flashes of towering cities made of crystal, oceans boiling beneath blood-red skies, and crowds frozen in place like statues, their lives paused mid-motion.

And then—silence.

A thud. Earth. Solid. Cold.

Isabella groaned as she rolled onto her back, blinking against the dizzying blur in her vision. She was lying on wet stone. Above her, the sky was dark, moonless, but tinged with an unnatural violet hue.

One by one, the others appeared, dropped unceremoniously beside her—Pablo, groaning and swearing in Spanish; Liberty, her glasses askew and her laptop bag miraculously intact; Camazotz, who landed on his feet with inhuman grace, silent as ever.

"Is everyone okay?" Isabella asked, her voice hoarse.

Liberty pushed herself up, brushing dust from her coat. "That was... different. I think we just got ejected from the Nexus into a splinter timeline."

"Define 'splinter,'" Pablo muttered, rubbing his shoulder.

"A reality that shouldn't exist. One formed from contradictions and paradoxes. Basically, a mistake," Liberty said.

Isabella got to her feet, tucking the glowing stone into her coat. Around them loomed the remnants of a city—once grand, now skeletal. Skyscrapers twisted at unnatural angles, streets flooded with fog that shimmered with iridescent energy. Time was broken here, suspended mid-moment. A shattered clock hovered in the air, its pieces frozen in mid-explosion.

"This place..." Camazotz's brow furrowed. "It's not just a mistake. It's a warning."

Isabella narrowed her eyes. "A warning of what?"

"The cost of tampering with time without balance," the wizard said grimly. "This is what happens when a Time Stone is misused."

Suddenly, the fog shifted. Out of it emerged figures—ghostly shapes, half-formed and flickering. They walked in loops, repeating motions like echoes of their former selves.

"Are those... people?" Liberty whispered.

"No," Camazotz said. "They are fragments. Shadows caught in paradox, trapped between what was and what never should've been."

They walked among the shadows in silence, the tension growing with each step. Isabella could feel the Esmeralda growing heavier in her pocket, its pulse syncing with her own heartbeat. It wanted something—no, needed something. She could feel it trying to guide her.

They followed the pull through the broken city, until they reached a plaza surrounded by fractured time monuments—statues of pharaohs beside astronauts, steam engines beside alien machines. And in the center, atop a dais of broken glass and bone, stood a familiar figure.

Judge Malcolm Rutherford.

Except... not quite.

He was younger here. Stronger. Wearing a dark coat laced with ancient markings and a crown of silver circuitry. His eyes glowed faintly with green energy—the unmistakable signature of the Time Stone.

"So," he said, his voice echoing unnaturally, "you've found your way to the Graveyard of Timelines. How poetic."

Isabella's hand shot to the stone. "You're not him. You're a version."

He chuckled. "I'm *what he will become*—should you fail. Should you hesitate." He gestured around. "This reality? My doing. This is what's possible when one stops caring about consequences."

Liberty stepped forward, glaring. "You're a remnant, a splinter self—an anomaly that shouldn't even exist. This whole timeline is unstable."

"Unstable?" Rutherford scoffed. "No, it's free. Free from rules. Free from judgment. That's what the Time Stone offers—ultimate choice."

Pablo growled, stepping beside Isabella. "You've destroyed everything here."

"Improvement is messy," Rutherford said. "But I've seen what's coming. The version of me you're fighting in the true timeline? He's on the verge of total control. And you—Isabella—you're running out of time."

He raised his hand, and the sky cracked.

Out of it poured entities of pure distortion—creatures made of static and warped light, their shrieks bending reality.

"Stop him!" Camazotz yelled, drawing a sigil into the air that flared with blue fire. "This version of Rutherford could destabilize the real timeline if left unchecked!"

The battle was chaos.

Liberty ducked behind a statue, hacking into the broken timeline using a makeshift temporal code, trying to find a weakness in the remnant Rutherford's control. Pablo charged forward with raw power, striking down one of the distortions with a roar. Camazotz summoned barriers of ancient magic to shield them, while Isabella—stone in hand—climbed the dais.

Rutherford watched her ascend. "You still don't understand the stone," he said. "It doesn't want to be *used*. It wants to *transform you*."

"Maybe," Isabella said, "but I'm not afraid of change."

She raised the Esmeralda high.

The light burst from it like a supernova—green, gold, and violet all at once—engulfing the plaza. Time screamed around them. The remnant Rutherford reached for her, but his form flickered, cracked, and crumbled into a spiral of dust.

The distortion creatures vanished.

The sky stitched itself back together.

And then—silence again.

The group stood panting in the center of the plaza, the monuments restored, the city flickering between ruin and renewal.

Isabella opened her eyes. The Esmeralda was glowing calmly now, as though it had passed a test of will.

"What did you do?" Liberty asked, awe in her voice.

"I accepted it," Isabella said quietly. "Not as a weapon. As a part of me."

Camazotz nodded, eyes filled with pride. "Then you're ready for what comes next."

She looked toward the horizon. Somewhere out there, in the real timeline, the true Rutherford still hunted them. But now, Isabella carried not just the stone—but understanding.

And she was no longer afraid.

Chapter 41: The Gathering Storm

The clouds above Manhattan swirled unnaturally, as if the sky itself were holding its breath.

Back in the real timeline, Isabella stood at the top of the Brooklyn Bridge, the Esmeralda de Tiempo pulsing steadily in her palm. It had been three days since their confrontation with the remnant Rutherford in the Graveyard of Timelines. Three days of silence, reflection, and anticipation.

Below, traffic crawled as usual, unaware that time itself teetered on the brink.

Liberty, seated cross-legged near a rusted maintenance beam, tapped at her keyboard, fingers dancing over holographic projections of collapsing timelines and tangled paradoxes. Her face was tight with focus, her usual cheer replaced by grim urgency.

"We've got less than seventy-two hours," she said, not looking up. "Rutherford's movements suggest he's preparing something big. Bigger than anything he's attempted before."

"How big?" Pablo asked, arms crossed, leaning on a girder like it was a barbell.

"Big enough to unravel the timeline from both ends," Liberty replied. "He's targeting the Moment of Convergence."

Isabella's brow furrowed. "What's that?"

Camazotz appeared beside her, his presence like a ripple through air. "It's the instant where all versions of the past, present, and future align—a temporal heartbeat. If disrupted, everything fractures. Time becomes untethered."

"Why would Rutherford do that?" Pablo asked. "Wouldn't he be destroyed too?"

"He doesn't care anymore," Isabella said quietly. "He wants absolute control—or total annihilation. Either way, he wins."

They were silent for a moment, the wind tugging at their jackets. Below, the hum of the city went on, oblivious.

"Where is he?" Isabella asked.

Liberty tapped a final key. A glowing map appeared above her laptop, marked by flickering red points of instability.

"Here," she said, pointing. "Washington, D.C. He's using the Supreme Court building as a focus. Symbolic and strategic."

Camazotz nodded. "Time converges there in two nights. We must act before then."

Pablo cracked his knuckles. "Then let's crash his party."

Isabella looked out over the city. She could feel it—the Esmeralda responding to the pulse of history. It vibrated with purpose now, not just power. It had chosen her, but it hadn't been an accident. Her struggles, her pain, her perseverance—it had all led to this.

"It's time," she said.

Liberty stood, packing her gear. "Road trip to save the universe?"

Isabella smiled faintly. "One last ride."

As they descended the bridge, the sky darkened with unnatural clouds. Storms brewed over the Capitol. Time rippled and twisted.

Rutherford was waiting.

And this time, the battle would decide everything.

Chapter 42: The Heart of the Convergence

The Supreme Court building loomed like a monument to judgment itself—its pillars towering under the storm-dark sky, the marble steps slick with rain that never seemed to touch the ground. Lightning flashed in unnatural patterns, illuminating cracks forming across reality itself. Time was unraveling.

Isabella stepped forward, Esmeralda de Tiempo in hand, glowing fiercely with emerald light. Camazotz walked beside her, his long coat fluttering behind him in the rising wind. Liberty, eyes scanning live holographic feeds, whispered coordinates and pressure points, while Pablo adjusted the gloves he'd reinforced with magnetized fiber-steel, ready for the inevitable brawl.

Inside, Judge Rutherford stood beneath the great rotunda, surrounded by the fractured timelines he'd brought into convergence. Dozens of versions of himself—some younger, some grotesquely altered— gathered in a circle, chanting ancient legal codes in tongues that had no place in this century.

In the center of it all, a temporal vortex twisted and burned, a swirling heart of golden-blue energy threatening to tear history apart.

"You came," Rutherford said, his voice layered with echoes of himself across time.

"We always do," Isabella said, stepping forward.

"You still believe you're meant to hold the Esmeralda? That a girl born into shadows, hunted by the law, could shape the timeline?" His smile was cold. "You don't belong here."

"I belong wherever truth does," she replied. "And the truth is, you're afraid."

Rutherford's eyes flared with temporal fire. "I am the law. I am time."

"No," Camazotz said, stepping forward, eyes glowing violet. "You are a man who lost everything and now seeks to destroy what others have."

Lightning exploded through the dome. One of Rutherford's doubles lunged—but Pablo intercepted him with a brutal strike, sending him sprawling through a vortex that closed around him like a steel trap.

Liberty unleashed a sonic beacon, freezing several alternate Rutherfords mid-motion. "You're outnumbered," she said, grinning.

Rutherford sneered. "I am *beyond* numbers."

The rotunda shifted, splitting into impossible geometries. Time fractured around them—Civil War soldiers marched through one corridor, while flying cars zipped past another. Screams, laughter, silence—all layered atop one another.

Isabella gripped the Esmeralda tighter. "We end this now."

She lifted the stone. Green light surged outward, slicing through the distortions. The vortex wailed.

"Isabella!" Liberty shouted. "Stabilize the core or the Convergence will collapse everything!"

"I need cover!"

Pablo leapt into the air, tackling a future-Rutherford armed with plasma cuffs. Camazotz chanted in a forgotten dialect, holding the vortex open just long enough for Isabella to step through.

Inside the core of the storm, time stood still. Her memories shimmered around her—her mother's voice, her first step in Chronic Bay, her first heartbreak, the first time she was called "illegal." All of it whispered around her like wind through trees.

"You were never meant to hold the Stone," came Rutherford's voice behind her. The *real* Rutherford. Scarred, tired, trembling with power.

"I wasn't *meant* for anything," Isabella said. "I *chose*."

She thrust the Esmeralda forward.

The Stone blazed.

History rewrote itself around her.

Chapter 43: The Vault of Broken Time

The cold air inside the ancient vault smelled of dust, metal, and forgotten memories. Isabella stepped forward slowly, each footfall echoing through the chamber like a ghost from the past. The walls were carved with glyphs—some Mayan, some unknown—each glowing faintly as if stirred by her presence. The Esmeralda pulsed in her hand, responding to the energy of the chamber.

"Careful," Camazotz warned, his voice low and reverent. "This place is a fracture in time itself. One wrong move could collapse entire timelines."

Liberty's eyes darted across the symbols, fingers flying over her holographic tablet. "I'm picking up dimensional interference. Whatever this place is—it's more than a vault. It's a convergence."

Behind them, Pablo kept a watchful eye on the entrance, his muscles taut. "Then let's not take any longer than we have to."

At the center of the vault stood a pedestal of obsidian, atop which hovered a crystalline dial—the Chronocore. Threads of light and shadow danced around it, whispering fragments of ancient voices. Isabella stepped closer. The Esmeralda vibrated more violently now, heat surging through her palm.

"The core is reacting to her," Camazotz said. "She's triggering the convergence."

Suddenly, time rippled. A gust of wind swept through the chamber, and the surroundings blurred—replaced by flashes of past lives, ancient wars, moments of joy and sorrow from a thousand years. Isabella gasped, stumbling back as visions clawed at her mind.

"I saw my mother," she whispered. "But she was… younger."

Liberty steadied her. "It's pulling memories from the stone. From you. It's not just showing history—it's testing your readiness."

Then came a voice—deep, smooth, and unnervingly familiar.

"You've come far, Isabella."

Judge Rutherford stepped from the shadows, clad in temporal armor shimmering like molten time. His eyes were cold, his expression unreadable.

"You were never meant to control the Esmeralda," he said. "You're a glitch in the design."

"Maybe," Isabella replied, lifting the stone, "but I'm here now. And I've seen enough to know you're not the guardian this power needs."

He smiled faintly. "Then prove you're worthy."

With a flick of his hand, time cracked open.

And the final trial began.

Chapter 44: Trial of the Timeless

The chamber shattered into fragments of space and memory.

One moment, Isabella was standing in the Vault of Broken Time— then the floor dropped beneath her feet. She spiraled through flashes of history: the Mexican countryside at dawn, neon-lit streets of future Tokyo, a child's room filled with laughter, a battlefield soaked in dust and blood.

Then: silence.

Isabella landed on her feet, breathless, in an endless white void. There was no sky. No ground. Only a horizon of glowing echoes stretching to eternity.

"You're in the trial," came Camazotz's voice, though he wasn't there.

"What do I do?" Isabella whispered.

The Esmeralda pulsed on her wrist, the gem now embedded in the fabric of her skin—alive with memory.

"Prove that you deserve time's favor," said a voice behind her.

Isabella turned to see a woman: cloaked in light, eyes like twin galaxies, hair braided with silver threads. She looked ancient and young all at once.

"Who are you?" Isabella asked.

"I am the Keeper of the Timeless Trial," the woman said. "Long ago, I too was tested by the Esmeralda. Now I guard its final secret."

Isabella steadied her breath. "Then test me."

The world shifted again.

Now she stood in her old apartment in Chronic Bay. Her mother sat at the table, folding laundry. A younger Isabella played in the corner, drawing stars with a broken crayon.

Her mother looked up and smiled. "Mija, stay. Just for tonight. Pretend none of this ever happened."

The air smelled like soap and tortillas.

"I can't," Isabella whispered.

"You *could*," the illusion said. "You could stay in this moment forever. Safe. Loved. Hidden."

Isabella walked to the door. "I didn't come this far to hide."

The room crumbled like dust.

Now: a courtroom.

Judge Rutherford stood above her, gavel raised.

"You are undocumented," he said. "A trespasser in time and law. How do you plead?"

Isabella stood tall. "Guilty... of surviving."

Rutherford slammed the gavel—but it shattered into light.

Now: blackness. She floated in it, suspended.

"You've passed," came the Keeper's voice, gentler now. "You've chosen courage over comfort. Truth over illusion."

A green flame ignited in the distance—then raced toward her.

When it struck, the Esmeralda burned like a second heart in her chest.

She gasped, falling to her knees as visions of all time—past, future, parallel—flooded her mind.

She saw Liberty building a time engine from scratch.

Pablo leading a rebellion in a fractured timeline.

Camazotz battling an ancient evil at the edge of the multiverse.

And she saw herself—older, wiser, walking through history like a living myth.

Isabella opened her eyes.

She was back in the Vault.

Camazotz helped her up, awe in his eyes. "You've changed."

"No," Isabella said, voice glowing with power. "I've become who I was meant to be."

Behind them, Rutherford growled.

"You've only unlocked the first door," he said. "There's still the matter of war."

Isabella turned to face him.

"Then let's finish what we started."

Chapter 45: The War That Shouldn't Exist

The Vault trembled as timelines collided, and the light from the Esmeralda danced across the walls in frantic pulses. Isabella stood at the center, the Time Stone now fully awakened, its energy woven through her bloodstream like cosmic fire. Across from her, Judge Malcolm Rutherford drew a blade made of pure chronosteel—its edges flickering through millennia.

"You've come far, Monteverdi," Rutherford said, his armor glinting with fragments of stolen history. "But you don't understand what's at stake. If you destroy me, you destroy the law that holds reality together."

Isabella's hands clenched into fists. "You never upheld the law. You twisted it. Used it to crush the powerless. I've seen what your version of time looks like—and I won't let it become our future."

Rutherford raised the blade. "Then die with your precious truth."

He charged.

Time shattered around them.

Isabella ducked, the blade slicing the air above her. Sparks burst from the impact, warping the floor into scenes from alternate lives—dozens of versions of Isabella flickering into view. A soldier. A mother. A queen. A corpse.

Camazotz summoned a barrier of golden runes just as Rutherford turned to strike again. "He's pulling power from the collapsed timelines!" the ancient wizard shouted. "You have to sever his tether to the Chronocore!"

Liberty appeared beside Isabella, holding a sleek device pulsing with blue light. "This'll get you in," she said, tossing it into Isabella's hand. "But you'll have to *will* the core to obey you. You're the only one who can overwrite his command."

"I know," Isabella said, eyes glowing.

She sprinted toward the pedestal, dodging Rutherford's attacks as the floor melted into scenes of destruction—New York in flames, Maya temples collapsing, the ruins of a future Earth overtaken by AI.

Pablo barreled into Rutherford with a roar, buying her time.

At the Chronocore, Isabella slammed the device into the pedestal. Light exploded outward, and a voice echoed in her mind: *"Isabella Monteverdi. Bearer of the Esmeralda. Do you claim authority over the flow of time?"*

"I do," she whispered, holding the stone to her chest. "Not to control it. To protect it."

"Then shape the path."

The core shattered—and time obeyed.

Reality slowed to a crawl. Rutherford's strike hung frozen in the air. The Vault began to dissolve into golden dust, the alternate timelines releasing their grip.

Isabella approached Rutherford, whose eyes flicked with confusion and rage even in slowed time.

She placed her hand on his chest.

"I'm not going to kill you," she said. "I'm going to show you what you've never seen."

She pressed the Esmeralda to his heart.

In an instant, Rutherford was flooded with every consequence of his actions—every unjust sentence, every life broken by his hand, every alternate world where he reigned like a tyrant.

He screamed.

And vanished.

The Vault crumbled.

Time healed.

And the Esmeralda dimmed, now quiet... for now.

The team stood in the remnants of the chamber, breathless.

"It's over," Camazotz said.

"No," Isabella said, staring at the dust in her palm. "It's just beginning."

Chapter 46: The Echo Beyond Time

A low hum filled the air, rhythmic like a heartbeat—only it wasn't coming from a person. It was the sound of time settling. After the collapse of the Vault and Rutherford's vanishing, the world around Isabella and her companions shimmered with the soft, golden haze of timelines realigning.

"We did it," Liberty said, blinking at the swirling energy around them. "I think we actually saved time."

Camazotz stepped forward, his gaze sweeping the chamber's remains. "We stopped *one* war. But the threads of time are delicate. Too much has changed too fast. There will be consequences."

Isabella turned toward the center of the fractured Vault, where the Esmeralda hovered, gently rotating. It no longer pulsed with wild energy—it hovered in perfect equilibrium, waiting.

"Then we'll deal with them," Isabella said. "Together."

Pablo clapped her on the shoulder. "You still haven't taken a breath, chica. Maybe we fix the multiverse... *after* tacos."

She laughed despite the ache in her chest. "Tempting."

But her eyes drifted back to the Esmeralda.

It began to drift toward her.

"I think… it's calling me again," she said softly.

Before anyone could respond, time itself split open once more.

But this time, it wasn't chaos—it was purpose.

A portal bloomed in the air before them, shimmering with green and silver light. Beyond it, they saw a realm untouched by history: floating islands suspended in twilight, giant crystal clocks ticking in silence, and constellations rearranging themselves like puzzle pieces.

"Where is that?" Liberty asked, stepping closer.

Camazotz's voice lowered. "That is the *Aeternum*—the space between all timelines. Only a true bearer of the Esmeralda may enter."

Isabella didn't hesitate. "Then that's where I'm going."

Pablo frowned. "Alone?"

"No," she said, turning to them. "Not alone. With all of you."

The team exchanged glances—nervous, excited, a little terrified—but each nodded.

Liberty adjusted her goggles. "I've already packed virtual snacks."

Camazotz smiled faintly. "I never thought I'd return. But fate has a curious sense of humor."

Pablo cracked his knuckles. "New realm, new enemies. Let's see what they've got."

Isabella took a deep breath, standing at the edge of the portal. Her past, her struggles, her doubts—they hadn't disappeared. But now, she had direction. She had power. She had family.

Together, they stepped into the Aeternum.

Behind them, the Vault faded into dust and stars.

Ahead of them, an infinite road unwritten.

Chapter 47: The Aeternum Paradox

The moment Isabella crossed into the Aeternum, her breath caught in her throat.

Time had no rules here.

The sky bent in impossible shapes, curving around itself in fluid spirals. Islands of floating stone drifted above an endless ocean of starlight. Clock towers hung upside down in the sky, their pendulums swinging to an unheard rhythm. Each tick echoed not just in the air—but in Isabella's chest, as though syncing with her heartbeat.

"This place is… alive," Liberty whispered, spinning slowly, awestruck. "I'm reading quantum data shifts every second. Time here isn't linear—it's layered."

"It's beautiful," Pablo muttered, then frowned. "But also hella creepy."

Camazotz nodded solemnly. "The Aeternum is the cradle of time. The Esmeralda was born here—crafted from collapsed futures and forgotten pasts. But be warned… what is sacred here is also deadly."

They stepped onto a bridge made of glowing script—ancient glyphs from every civilization Isabella had ever studied, and many she hadn't. Each step seemed to take them forward and backward simultaneously, the horizon shifting with every breath.

Suddenly, a voice boomed through the air—not heard, but *felt* in their minds.

"Bearer of the Esmeralda. Why have you come?"

A figure formed in the distance, coalescing from fractured constellations: tall, robed in shadow and starlight, eyes like burning clocks.

"The Chronarch," Camazotz said softly. "He's the guardian of the Aeternum. I hoped he was a myth."

Isabella stepped forward, heart steady. "I came to restore balance. The Stone was misused—fracturing the timeline, unraveling worlds. I want to repair what's been broken."

The Chronarch tilted his head. "One does not *repair* time. One lives through its consequences."

"But I have the Esmeralda," she said, lifting it from her chest. "I can help—"

"Power does not grant wisdom," the Chronarch interrupted. "Before you shape time, you must first understand *your* place in it."

He raised a hand—and reality *fractured*.

Isabella screamed as she was pulled into a vortex of memory and possibility. Her friends vanished. The Aeternum dissolved into shards of her life:

—She was ten again, crossing the border in the back of a truck.
—She was twenty-three, hiding from ICE agents in a grocery store freezer.
—She was thirty, standing trial in Rutherford's court.
—She was *dead*, forgotten in a world where no one ever found the Esmeralda.

Each vision slammed into her like a wave, suffocating her.

And then… silence.

She stood alone in a version of New York City frozen in time. Buildings hung mid-collapse. People stood mid-breath, unmoving. A mirror appeared before her.

She stepped toward it.

But her reflection wasn't her.

It was *another* Isabella—worn, angry, corrupted by power. She wore the Esmeralda around her neck like a trophy. Her eyes were empty.

"I became what I hated," the reflection said. "Is that what you want?"

"No," Isabella whispered. "I want to protect them. I want to choose better."

The reflection nodded—and stepped back into the mirror.

The world reformed.

Isabella stood once more before the Chronarch, now kneeling, breathless but whole.

He stared down at her, silent.

Then, finally, he spoke.

"Then you may begin."

The glyph bridge expanded, revealing seven gates—each one shimmering with a different hue of time.

Camazotz, Liberty, and Pablo appeared at her side again, their faces showing the same realization: they'd each been tested too.

Isabella looked forward. "Let's fix the world. All of them."

They stepped toward the first gate.

Chapter 48: Gates of the Fractured Hour

The seven gates before them shimmered like living auroras, each pulsing with a color that sang a distinct note—a chord strung through time itself. They weren't just portals. They were *trials*. Echoes of broken timelines in need of repair.

Isabella stood at the edge of the bridge, her breath frosting in the strange, timeless air. The Esmeralda de Tiempo glowed warmly against her chest. It no longer felt like a weapon, or even a relic. It felt like a part of her.

Camazotz stepped beside her. "Each gate leads to a world warped by imbalance. A timeline poisoned by the misuse—or absence—of the Esmeralda's influence."

"Seven timelines," Liberty murmured, tapping on her holographic interface. "And we don't know which order matters, or what waits inside."

Pablo cracked his knuckles. "Doesn't matter. We handle it one punch, one plan at a time."

Isabella smiled faintly. "Then let's start with the one that calls loudest."

The gate glowing with deep crimson flared.

Without hesitation, they stepped through.

Timeline One: The Scarlet Reign (1467 – Renaissance Florence)

The air shifted, and they emerged in a smoky hall of mirrors—ornate and gold-trimmed, but covered in soot and ash. Outside, Florence burned. The skyline was choked in black clouds, and above the city floated something impossible—a mechanical throne carried by winged automatons.

From it, *Leonardo da Vinci* ruled—not as an artist or scientist, but as a tyrant.

"He shouldn't be like this," Liberty whispered, her eyes wide. "He was meant to be a genius, yes—but a humanist, a dreamer, not a dictator."

"They twisted him," Camazotz growled. "Someone gave him knowledge too soon. He harnessed steam and electricity before the world was ready."

"Which means," Isabella said, "we need to take it back."

They split up—Pablo and Liberty to disable the throne's core; Isabella and Camazotz to confront da Vinci directly.

Inside his palace, da Vinci wore an exosuit of brass and lightning. His face was beautiful, but eyes cold as mercury. "You seek to erase my gift," he said, voice echoing with artificial power. "The Esmeralda showed me the future. I only accelerated it."

"You enslaved half of Europe," Isabella shot back. "That's not progress. That's control."

"I offered unity," he snarled. "The same as your precious Judge Rutherford."

That name lit a fire in Isabella's chest. She lifted the Esmeralda, letting its energy pulse outward. "And like him, you'll fall."

The battle was brief but brutal—Pablo and Liberty sabotaging the throne's engine as Isabella unleashed a temporal echo, showing Leonardo what his dream could have been: a Florence where invention elevated humanity, not ruled it.

Leonardo's exosuit cracked. His throne sputtered. The sky cleared.

The timeline shimmered, righting itself.

As the gate reopened to the Aeternum, da Vinci—now a quiet man again—whispered, "Forgive me."

Isabella nodded. "In time."

Back in the Aeternum, the crimson gate dimmed. Six remained.

"Where next?" Liberty asked.

Camazotz closed his eyes. "The next most broken."

A cobalt gate surged open—its sound like glass cracking.

Without speaking, they stepped through once more.

Chapter 49: Echoes in the Snow

The cold hit them first—sharp and immediate, like shards of time themselves piercing through skin. They had landed in a frozen world, though it was not the Ice Age nor any known glacial period. Snow spiraled from a violet sky, falling in slow, deliberate flurries, as though time itself had grown tired.

Isabella pulled her jacket tighter as the Esmeralda glowed faintly beneath it. "This doesn't feel like Earth."

"It isn't," Camazotz said gravely. "Not anymore. This timeline fractured so severely, it folded space along with time. This is a dead Earth... from a possible future."

Liberty's scanners whirred to life. "There's no sun. No rotation. The planet is stuck in permanent twilight, orbit broken. How is this even—"

She stopped, eyes wide as figures emerged from the mist. Not people. Echoes.

Dozens of translucent, whispering forms drifted across the snow, each frozen in mid-action—laughing, crying, dancing. Ghosts caught in the last moments before the timeline shattered.

One reached for Isabella. Its fingers passed through her, but left behind a whisper: *Stop the flood... before the sixth bell.*

"What flood?" Pablo asked, hand tightening around the grip of his machete.

Camazotz narrowed his eyes. "The collapse. Some act... some decision... triggered the chain reaction that pulled this planet out of orbit and into decay. We're looking at the result of a timeline where climate manipulation became a weapon."

They traced the source to an abandoned compound half-buried beneath the snow. Inside: broken satellites, shattered greenhouses, and a control panel still glowing with warnings in seven languages.

Liberty moved to the console. "This was a weather regulation array. But the last command wasn't regulation—it was a trigger."

She brought up a hologram of a woman: young, powerful, desperate. A scientist. *Dr. Nadira Bell.*

"She tried to reverse climate collapse by seizing control from world governments. But her override destabilized the core. Earth's rotation stopped."

Camazotz nodded solemnly. "A brilliant heart, misled by fear."

They had a choice: travel back to before Nadira's command, or confront her temporal echo now—locked in a loop of regret and fury.

"I'll speak to her," Isabella said. "She needs to see what her choice did."

Within the shattered greenhouse, Nadira's echo stood, surrounded by withered plants. When Isabella approached, the echo turned—and the past and future collided.

"You came to judge me?" Nadira asked. "Or to change me?"

"To remind you of what hope looks like," Isabella said, lifting the Esmeralda.

She channeled an image—not just of survival, but rebirth. Earth healing, not through control, but cooperation. Her power reached Nadira's echo, not with force, but with grace.

The frozen wind softened. The sky lightened.

The timeline trembled—and began to correct.

They emerged from the gate as it dimmed behind them. Two down. Five remained.

Pablo looked to Isabella. "What happens when we reach the last gate?"

She didn't answer at first. Then: "We'll face him."

Judge Rutherford.

And the moment that would decide everything.

Chapter 50: The Eye of the Storm

The Time Gate flared with blinding emerald light as Isabella stepped through, the Esmeralda clutched tightly in her hand. Her companions followed—Camazotz with a heavy silence, Liberty scanning ahead with trembling hands, and Pablo tightening the straps of his vest like a man preparing for war.

They had arrived in Washington, D.C., but not as they knew it. The skyline was twisted—monuments replaced with gleaming spires, each etched with a single symbol: the scales of justice, cracked down the middle.

"This isn't our present," Liberty whispered. "It's a version of now... if Rutherford had seized the Stone."

The air shimmered with energy. Chrono-sentinels—humanoid machines infused with fragments of the Time Stone—patrolled the streets, scanning for deviations in the timeline. Each wore black judicial robes over reinforced armor. Each carried gavel-shaped scepters that could bend time in small, brutal bursts.

Camazotz gestured toward the Capitol building, now floating several meters above the ground, suspended by a network of gravitational rings. "He's there. Waiting."

As they moved through the war-torn city, Isabella saw echoes of people she once knew—faces from past timelines twisted by Rutherford's influence. The justice system had become prophecy: crimes judged before they were committed, people sentenced for futures they hadn't yet lived.

"This is what he wants," Pablo said. "A world where control is total. Where fear writes the law."

At the base of the Capitol, they were met by a figure in a silver cloak: the last of the temporal seers. She bowed to Isabella.

"You are late, but not too late."

"What happens if we fail?" Isabella asked.

The seer pointed upward. "Time will collapse into a single, eternal verdict. No choice. No chance. Only judgment."

They ascended the spiral of light that led into the levitating Capitol. Inside: silence. Hallways lined with portraits of alternate realities. Timelines where Isabella never found the Stone. Where Camazotz died centuries ago. Where Pablo returned to prison and Liberty never escaped her lab.

Rutherford waited in the rotunda, seated on a throne built from old law books and broken clocks. He wore a robe stitched from verdicts, his eyes glowing with the corrupted essence of the Time Stone.

"You made it," he said, voice like a verdict. "Now stand trial."

Isabella stepped forward. "We don't answer to you."

"No," Rutherford said. "You answer to time. And I am its executioner."

The room erupted into chaos.

Rutherford summoned waves of temporal distortion—rewinding moments, pausing others, fast-forwarding reality itself. Camazotz blocked the first onslaught with ancient magic, but even he faltered under the Stone's weight. Liberty hacked into the chrono-grid, short-circuiting the throne's anchor field. Pablo broke through Rutherford's defenses with brute force, buying Isabella the seconds she needed.

She held the Esmeralda high. It pulsed with everything she had learned, seen, and become. It wasn't just a weapon—it was a story. Her story.

And with a cry, she cast the light toward Rutherford.

The power struck him—not to destroy, but to *reveal*. His illusions collapsed. His strength faded. The throne crumbled beneath him, and for the first time, Judge Malcolm Rutherford looked afraid.

"You... you don't know what you've done," he said.

"Yes," Isabella whispered, stepping closer. "I gave time back to the people."

The rotunda dissolved into white light.

Time reset.

The Capitol returned to its rightful place. The chrono-sentinels vanished. Across the world, timelines recalibrated. The Stone dimmed, no longer needed—but still held by one who understood its cost.

Outside, the city breathed again.

Pablo slung his bag over his shoulder. "So... we win?"

"We begin," Camazotz said softly.

Liberty looked to Isabella. "What now?"

Isabella smiled. "Now we fix what's left. Together."

The Esmeralda pulsed once more—quiet, gentle, and at peace.

Chapter 51: The Ripple Beyond Time

The dust of victory had not yet settled when Isabella awoke with a start, the Esmeralda pulsing faintly under her palm. The early morning light filtered through the sheer curtains of the safehouse they had found in Chronic Bay—a modest apartment tucked above a corner bodega where time, for once, seemed still.

She looked around. Liberty was asleep on a beanbag chair, surrounded by printouts and wires from a partially disassembled drone. Pablo snored softly on the couch, an empty protein bar wrapper balanced on his chest. Camazotz sat by the window, silhouetted against the dawn, reading a leather-bound book that hadn't existed yesterday.

Something in Isabella's chest ached—not pain, exactly, but a tug. A reminder.

"We changed the future," she whispered.

Camazotz didn't look up. "You stabilized a branch. But time is not linear, Isabella. It folds. Breathes. Remembers."

She frowned. "What do you mean?"

"The Esmeralda did more than defeat Rutherford. It unraveled a knot that should have never existed. But when you pull a single thread in a tapestry—"

"You risk unraveling the rest," she finished.

A knock at the door interrupted them.

Pablo sat up instantly, reaching for the bat he kept beside him. Liberty stirred, blinking awake.

Isabella answered.

Standing in the hall was a young woman—no older than Liberty—with wide eyes and trembling hands. She held a box sealed with old wax and markings Isabella recognized instantly: ancient Mayan.

"This is for you," the girl said. "They told me you'd know what to do."

"Who told you?" Isabella asked gently.

"The ones from the dream," the girl whispered. "The ones who watch through time."

Camazotz rose like a shadow behind her. "Pregivers."

Isabella took the box. It was heavier than it looked. Inside, wrapped in silken cloth, was a second stone—translucent, violet, and vibrating with quiet power.

Liberty peered over her shoulder. "Another Time Stone?"

"No," Camazotz said, touching the box reverently. "This is something... older. Wiser. A memory fragment from the First Dawn."

The violet gem shimmered, and images flashed across the room—civilizations long dead, stars collapsing in silence, forgotten gods weeping at the edge of eternity.

Pablo whistled. "What now? More time travel?"

Isabella held the stone up, and it hummed softly in her hand, syncing with the Esmeralda.

"I think this is something else," she said slowly. "Not a journey through time... but through *truth*."

Camazotz nodded. "The past was one battlefield. The mind, the soul, the heart—that is the next."

Liberty grabbed her laptop. "You're telling me there's another layer?"

"A deeper one," Isabella said. "We've saved the world as it was. Now we find out why it broke to begin with."

The stone pulsed.

Far away—in a world outside of time—an unseen figure smiled in the dark.

La Esmeralda de Tiempo

Made in the USA
Monee, IL
01 May 2025

7ac7818f-2f04-41f4-a5de-ea25ee5774e0R01